THE CONGO

THE CONGO

Where Men Are Eaten

Juan Rodriguez

 **New Generation Publishing**

CONTENTS

Juan Rodríguez

THE SPANISH LEGION

1952-1955

The seeds of my adventure were sown and starting to germinate when I was a boy of eleven in Madrid, Spain.

I spent my time, when I wasn't at school, playing in the streets around *Estrecho* with other boys from the neighbourhood.

At this time, there was plenty of liberty for the children whose fathers had died in the Spanish Civil War, the year being 1936.

Mother found it very difficult, trying to bring up six children, who were aged between seven and nineteen, all on her own. My father was dying and my mother had the worry of that; also, there was little money, his having been the only source of income, which was soon to peter out.

My mother told the elder brothers that they would have to find work, which was very hard at that time, and the eldest of the children was my sister, Elisa, who was at school, in a convent, obtaining an education paid for by a nun. It was to enable her to get a good job in the future.

My elder brothers, because they hadn't received much education, as their studies had to be cut short in order to go out and earn money to help pay for the basic essentials, were unqualified for any skilled work, and therefore, the only jobs available to them were cafeteria jobs, fetching and carrying in a hotel, or odd jobs in a bar, for which the pay was very low. But even so, one was grateful to be able to obtain even one of these lowly paid jobs.

By this time, my mother had told me that I also would have to get a job, as the extra money was needed, so I had to leave school at the age of eleven. It was not a matter of trying to get the permission of the education authorities at those times. Nobody prevented you. Many people were in similar circumstances at that time. Food for the stomach was given priority over education.

I found myself a job, in one week, in a bar-cafeteria of a high standard, which only business people frequented. The proprietor of the establishment told me that I was very young and that the only vacancy for me was that of a pageboy; the work consisted of having to get taxis, fetching cigarettes, giving messages by letter to people around Madrid, for which I would have to go on the underground station, where I lost myself more than once, also fetching tickets for a bullfight, and so on.

I worked from nine in the morning until two thirty in the afternoon, and from six thirty until ten thirty at night. On days that my colleagues had days off, I had to work right through without being allowed to go home for a break. My mother, on these occasions, used to bring me something to eat from home. She would drop it into the hotel for me, and I used to eat when I got the opportunity, downstairs, in the washing-up room.

The pay was very low, but I used to get tips, which amounted to around ten to fifteen pesetas a day, which wasn't bad in those days, as the money then had much more buying power.

I met some well-known celebrities during the time I worked there. For example, the number one bullfighter, named Julio Aparicio, also, Miguel Baez El Litri, Gitanillo de Triana, and Antonjio Ordonez. These top-drawer matadors used to come to the cafeteria to discuss contracts.

It was very exciting for me meeting these important people, especially being a young, impressionable boy. They were instrumental in my seeking a future that offered adventure, a taste for the good things in life, and also, excitement, which I craved, and never more so than when I was totally bored with the mundane tasks at my place of employment, which I accepted, however, as a means to an end.

Juan Rodriguez—1947—aged 11

Sometimes, other pageboys, from other cafeterias, would arrange to meet at a coffee shop close by to play a game of billiards or smoke a cigarette. The latter was not forbidden, this being one of the things that youngsters of that particular time acquired the habit of through lack of firm parental control.

Four years passed; I was working at this same bar-cafeteria, and during that time, my father died. My mother was heartbroken, and it was the first time I had seen a dead person. The fact that it was someone so close and personal made it all the more frightening and a terrible shock to bear.

A little while after my father's death, my brothers and I had more freedom. I then moved to another bar-cafeteria named the 'Congosto', in the road called Aduana, in the centre of Madrid. It was a promotion for me because I was allowed to serve behind the bar. People liked to come here and select their own fresh fish and shellfish from the front of the premises, where it was displayed. They would wait for it to be cooked and eat it accompanied by wines or beer, I remember. It was a very popular place and always very busy.

I made friends with another boy who worked at the 'Congosto'; he was two years elder than me. He was more experienced than I was, and he used to take me to places of entertainment and also to look for girls.

I soon got fed up with this, as the spending money was going too rapidly, and I was finding that after a night out with Luis, I was broke the next day.

I realised that this was no good for me, and I wasn't making any progress. My thoughts were engrossed in adventure. This is what I had a yearning for, and I knew that it had to be satisfied.

By now, I was feeling uncertain and dissatisfied, and I was wondering how I could get away from Madrid, to find something new and exciting to do, or a better job, which would pay more, and enable me to give more to my mother than I was able to do at that time.

The next day, I left the house and was walking towards the underground station; on my way to work, suddenly, I recognised a boy from my neighbourhood.

He was struggling with a woman and trying to take her handbag from her, which he succeeded in doing. He then ran away with it and left the woman screaming, 'That boy has taken my money.' I remembered him as being one of the boys that I had played with, many times, around the streets when I was younger.

I was amazed to witness what had happened but could do nothing about it, as he had disappeared out of sight, into the next street, apparently.

A few days later, on my next day off from work, I went out into the street and saw a group of boys, who I knew, sitting on the pavement, playing cards for money. Who should be there amongst them but the boy who had robbed the woman of her handbag?

He called to me, 'Hello, Juan. Where are you going?' To which I replied, 'It's my day off and I am going to see if I can find someone I know, to go into town with, for a drink and chat.'

'Oh, good', he said. 'I'll come with you.' And after he had thrown down some pesetas to his friends, we set off together. But he didn't want to go into the centre of Madrid, as he had friends working in a bar close by.

Having ordered the drinks, I started to pay, but Luis would not let me. 'No, it's OK,' he said. 'I have plenty of money. I'll pay.'

He took a pile of money from his pocket and paid the barman and also gave him a good tip. I was surprised at the amount of money he had and asked him, 'Where did you get all that money from? Is that the money you took from that woman's handbag a few days ago?'

'No,' he replied. 'I earned this money, working.'

'Don't tell lies,' I said to him. 'I saw what you did, with that lady's bag.' 'Yes, that's right,' he told me afterwards. 'But I'm not working, and I have to get money from somewhere, to live.'

'Do you do this sort of thing, all the time then?' I asked. Luis replied that he was unskilled for a job. And also that he had been in a reform school twice. He had no father, and things were difficult for his mother, so he had to give her money to buy the food.

'Anyway, Juan, forget that,' he said to me. 'Let's go somewhere else now and have a good time.' He offered to pay for everything.

I was a bit scared, now having this knowledge of him being a pickpocket. 'Don't do this business when I'm with you,' I told him. 'I'll only go with you on that condition. Because if you get caught doing it when I'm with you, I will get into trouble as well!'

'I promise not to,' Luis said. So we left the bar and caught a taxi to the city centre, where he said he had to do something important. We arrived at a place called 'Lavapies', where there were some women near the underground, selling flowers and cigarettes.

Luis approached one of the women, who he apparently knew. He spoke to her, for a few minutes, in a secretive fashion. Then he took some money from his pocket and gave some to the woman for which she, in turn, handed him cigarettes.

Luis came back to where I was standing, waiting for him to finish his conversation. He took me by the arm and said hurriedly, 'Come on, Juan, we're going to have a smoke. These are special and make you feel happy.'

I asked him what they were. And he told me that they were a drug from Morocco, called kifi, and said not to be afraid to smoke one because they were not very strong.

I hadn't had any experience of drugs previously of any description. And after smoking one, I became sort of carefree, with my words flowing freely. As we talked, we laughed. All the tension seemed to have evaporated, and I had never known any of these sensations before.

Luis took me into another bar close by, where there were Spanish gipsies, singing, dancing, and clapping their hands. He called one of his friends over to me and told the gipsy to sing for us. The flamenco singer was happy to oblige. As Luis was paying him, we stayed there for two hours or more. We then made our way to the underground station, which was full of people, and we had to weave our way through. We caught a train back to 'Estrecho', and when we had got out of the tube station, Luis then told me, 'Look at this.' He showed me hundreds of pesetas in his hand.

I said to him, 'You told me you wouldn't do that again when you were with me. You promised, and now you have broken your word, by doing it again, already.'

I was angry and disgusted with Luis; that he could break his word to me so easily meant that there was no depth of feeling in him. I walked away from him, leaving him standing there in the street. He made no attempt to follow me, and I went home.

One week later, I read in the newspaper that Luis had been arrested and taken to prison to serve a lengthy sentence. When I ran into his mother in the street, sometime later, I asked her about Luis, and she said that she was very upset by the business and that he had to stay in prison for another three years, as he had more than one conviction of these charges.

It was April now, and I was looking for a job on the coast in Spain. I was lucky enough to find a job for six months in the Hotel Inglaterra, in San Sebastian, which was situated in the Basque territory.

I enjoyed myself working at this place of high standard and learned the complete procedure of the restaurant. I was sixteen by now, and I met some very nice people in the hotel. For example, a group of flamenco dancers and singers, of high repute, named Miguel de los Reyes. They were appearing at the best theatre, in San Sebastian, and they gave tickets to me and my friends to go and see them in their show.

When the six months had passed, I went back home to Madrid, as I was once more in the position of having to find work. My mother was happy to see me and so were my brothers. I reassured her that I would find something. But I, myself, felt that I was back at square one, without having progressed.

My mother asked me why I was always changing jobs. I told her that I was looking for adventure, and I couldn't help the fact that it was uppermost in my mind.

Shortly after my return to Madrid, I bumped into a former childhood friend from this locality, where we grew up. His name was Antonio; he also lost his father, in the war. He had a younger brother, who was mentally handicapped, and their mother had to go out to work and earn money to support them.

I remember vividly, how, as a young boy, Antonio's ambition was to be a famous matador (torero). We used to go into the fields so that Antonio could practise his bullfighting skill until he had reached the grace of using the cape, precision with the sword, and so on so that he would not get killed but be hero-worshipped by the people.

He was very pleased to see me, and it had been two years or more since we were together.

'Are you a matador yet?' I asked Antonio.

He replied, 'No, Juan. It's very difficult, but I have to kill two bulls next week. It's a recommendation by a friend. I have to go to Segovia, and my expenses are being paid. If you want to come with me, you can. We can stay in a guest house, where we will meet the president of the bullfighting association of Segovia. They are having a fete, for a week, there, and I would be glad of your company.'

'That is very exciting,' I said. 'I don't have any money at the moment. But if you say that it is being paid for and not out of your own pocket, then I would like to come and watch you and see the spectacle.'

The prospect was thrilling, and when we arrived at Segovia on the train, I was amazed to see such a crowd of people, waiting for the young matador to arrive. The president of the bullfighting association approached Antonio and shook him by the hand. He then shook my hand, as by, this time; I had been introduced as a friend.

The president then asked us to follow him to the main road, where the house that we were to stay in was situated.

It was quite a noisy trip from the station, as we were followed by a group of people, fifty or more, shouting 'viva el matador'.

We checked our luggage into the guest house, and then the president invited Antonio and me to take a glass of wine with him in a little bar further down the street. After which, he took us along to where the bulls were kept so that Antonio could have a look at the two bulls he had to kill the following day.

After that, we were taken to see some of the sights of Segovia with the president and some friends of his. We enjoyed a very good dinner at the guest house and we retired to bed so that Antonio could get sufficient sleep and feel fresh and alert for his task the next day.

In the morning, we did our preparation and had a good breakfast. We went out to pass the time, as the corrida was not taking place until four o'clock in the afternoon. There was a happy and exciting atmosphere everywhere as the anticipation of the bullfight was getting to the people by this time. They loved the danger and the thrill of it all.

Boys and girls were coming up to us and wanting to shake Antonio's hand, and they shook my hand also, though I didn't know why. I was only going to be a spectator.

Several times Antonio was asked if he was nervous, having to kill the bulls. To which he replied, 'No, I'm not afraid. I am very happy to be here today. I have been practising for this moment for a long time. I will entertain you once I get into the arena, and you won't be disappointed.'

The time for the corrida to commence was fast approaching now. We had been enjoying ourselves, but the time was near for Antonio to gather his thoughts together for the serious business that was at hand. Any lack of concentration on his part could mean a nasty accident, whereby he could be the victim. And no doubt, his childhood ambition and dreams of being a famous matador could be shattered for all time.

The two bulls that Antonio had selected to kill were strong, angry, and just waiting to be let loose. Antonio was, by now, back at the guest house, changing into his costume, which was given to him by the president.

I helped him to dress in his regalia, and, as he stood there in front of the mirror, all in bright blue and yellow, his face was a picture of pride, which I knew I wouldn't forget. And so that Antonio would have this moment recorded for the future, he took out a camera from his case and asked me to take a photograph of him, which I did. I took more, some when we were in the street, and then again, when he had climbed on to the carriage, which had been sent, especially for him. Antonio was so happy, his face rippled with happiness and excitement at the prospect of fulfilling his longest remembered ambition.

We arrived at the arena and waited behind the barriers until the first bull that Antonio had to kill was released into the centre ring. He handed me his muleta to keep for him until he needed to use it. He was to use the big cape first of all. Antonio looked towards the bulls, and at that moment, the signal was given to the man in charge to open the gate and let the first bull out.

Antonio entered the ring and immediately went into action with his cape, twirling it around and showing his fancy footwork. This had the people shouting out ole, ole, and the atmosphere quickly started to build up with interest for this young, new-to-the-game matador.

Whilst the beast was at the other end of the arena, Antonio took advantage of the moment to race over to where I was in order to take the muleta and the sword, which I had been keeping ready for him, from my hands and as he did so said to me, 'Watch, Juan, you will see what I have been practising, all this time. The skill of the hand movements to deceive the bull.' And he was gone from me to do just as he had said.

I stood there numb and amazed as I watched Antonio approach the bull, saying to it, 'Hey, Toro,' and again, 'Hey, Toro.'

There was no hesitancy, and Toro replied by charging towards his enemy, who was waiting very calmly to confuse Toro with the swirling of the muleta, which concealed the sword. Antonio took the bull to the right and then to the left as he changed hands, and he was getting a loud ovation from the people.

His movements were as graceful as a ballerina, and the bull was getting a little tired by now. It was in this well-judged moment that Antonio decided to make the kill. With the muleta in his left hand and the sword in his right hand, Antonio stood momentarily still while he gazed at the bull intently. The beast had his head slightly lowered, as if it was deciding what move to make. But then, Antonio pointed the sword behind the animal's head, and quickly and decisively, he thrust the steel deep into the vulnerable spot. The bull struggled for a moment or two, thrashing his head this way and that and moved as if in a drunken daze, before toppling over, dead, with blood pouring from its mouth.

Antonio stood over the unfortunate beast, with satisfaction clearly on his face, and his right arm raised in the air to signal his victory.

The people were well satisfied and were screaming out to show their delight. Antonio came over to me, with happiness on his face. I congratulated him and told him what a good job he had done. I told him that he was a real matador.

At that moment, two horses with a cart behind and two men went over to the dead bull to remove it from the arena. The spectators were, by this time, throwing money into the ring as their appreciation for the way in which they had been entertained. Many of them were standing, vociferously, and some were waving their handkerchiefs.

I went into the arena to help Antonio collect all the pesetas and euros which had been thrown down for him. And I did not know until then, that this was the only way, in which Antonio was to be paid. But it was as much as if he had been paid a set fee.

Antonio told me to hold on to the money for him because after fifteen minutes' rest, he had to go out into the ring again to kill his second bull.

Antonio went through, more or less, the same procedure, showing his bravery towards the angered beast, which charged at him and caught him by the leg, with its horns, and tossed Antonio to the ground but not before he had been lifted slightly into the air.

As soon as I saw that Antonio had been hurt, I came out from behind the barrier, where I had been watching, and without realising what I was doing, I waved the cape frantically to distract the animal, and therefore give Antonio a moment to regain his composure.

My friend was not seriously hurt, and he had already risen from the ground. He called to me, 'Juan, Juan, leave him to me. It's all right. Leave him to me. Go quickly.'

I did as I was instructed and returned hurriedly behind the barrier. And it was only then that I fully realised just what I had done. It had been an instinctive act at a moment when I thought that my friend had been in danger.

It was not long afterwards that Antonio completed his task for the second time and killed the bull. And this time, the ovation from the crowd was even stronger and more appreciated, as he had been wounded, and the blood could be seen through Antonio's torn trousers.

A few youths had gathered around him and were now lifting Antonio up on to their shoulders. They continued carrying him out into the streets, which surrounded the bullring across the main road and back to the guest house where we were staying.

I took hold of Antonio's bodyweight, supporting him from under the arm, as he was limping. Somebody from behind said, 'Quickly sit him down in the chair so that I can look at his leg. I am the doctor from the infirmary.'

After the doctor had inspected Antonio's leg, the verdict was that there was a shallow cut, which he disinfected and stitched there and then. 'The bruise would heal in a few days,' he told Antonio and after he had congratulated the matador, left the house.

The president of the bullfighting association arrived to see Antonio and to make sure that all was well. After congratulating my friend about his work in the arena, he took an envelope from his breast pocket and handed it to Antonio, saying, 'This is for you. Everybody has contributed in a collection, and we are all very pleased with your work. If you want to come again next year, let me know. You will be welcome!' He then shook Antonio's hand and mine and said goodbye.

After about half an hour, we packed our things together and made our way to the railway station to catch the train back to Madrid.

On our arrival, we then took a taxi to Antonio's house. His mother and brother greeted him warmly, obviously happy to see him again. His mother was concerned about the bandage on Antonio's leg, but he assured her it was nothing to worry over.

She soon departed to the kitchen, insisting that I stay and eat with them, which I did, as, by this time, I was hungry. As we ate the meal and talked about the afternoon's events, Antonio handed me a few hundred pesetas, thanking me for my help and company.

I was reluctant to take the money, but Antonio insisted, and he told me he would like us to do it again sometime. But that the problem was, not having many influential people in the business, to keep him going. I told him I would gladly help him, if ever I was in a position to do so.

When it was time for me to leave his house, Antonio and his mother stood at the front door to see me off. His mother had tears in her eyes, as Antonio and I had been childhood friends of long-standing. I remember Antonio laughing, as we shook hands for the final time, not realising that we would never meet again.

I made my way home by foot, as the distance between our houses was just a comfortable walk. Or maybe it was just the frame of mind that I was in, at that particular moment, and couldn't be bothered to wait for a bus.

My mother, in turn, was relieved on my arrival home. She wanted to know how things had gone at the corrida, and I was then subjected to a battery of questions, which I had to answer, before she would let me relax.

After I had explained everything that had taken place that afternoon, she then said, 'I don't understand you, Juan. You're always going on some adventure or other. Whenever you leave the house, I never know when I would be able to see you again.'

The next day, I went into the centre of Madrid to look once more for a job. I made the rounds of all the hotels, but there was no vacancy for me, and I finished up feeling completely frustrated, with practically no money in my pocket.

I didn't know what to do with myself. I was thinking that maybe there would be a better chance for me if I could leave Spain and get to a country where there were more jobs to be had, as I couldn't go on like this.

I turned things over in my mind and realised the impossibilities of my desire at that particular time. My age was against me, and I couldn't get a passport till I had done my Spanish Military Service. So, after making enquiries, the only way open to me was to volunteer at the age of seventeen to join the Spanish Foreign Legion or wait until I was twenty-one before I could join the regular army, which conscripted men of that age.

As I couldn't get a job, I was passing the time doing nothing of interest or importance but just going out with casual friends, whose main quest was looking for girls and drinking in the bars and cafeterias. I decided at the spur of the moment, and without telling anyone, not even my mother, to go and join the recruitment flag of the Spanish Legion.

I arrived at the main entry gates of the building, and there were two Spanish sentinels on guard. They were fully fledged Spanish Legionnaires, armed with guns.

I was nervous and, at the same time, excited. I walked backwards and forwards, past the heavy iron gates, for what seemed like ten or fifteen minutes, uncertain as to what exactly I should do next. But I will never forget how heavily my heart was pounding in my chest.

This was one of those times when a person feels alone, as they are about to make a tremendously important and daring decision in their life, wondering if it will be for the good, or if they will regret it. And for someone who had never been far from their home, it was, in its way, a little frightening.

I studied the uniforms of the legionnaires, who showed pride, judging by the expression on their faces, and I admired them, in their green uniforms.

It was the feeling of admiration that dispelled my understandable nervousness. My adventurous spirit took hold of me then, and without any further hesitation, I walked through the main gates only to be stopped immediately by one of the legionnaires, who, I noticed, had the stripes on his sleeves, denoting that he held the rank of a corporal.

He asked me where I was going, and I told him that I was going to volunteer to become a legionnaire.

He then asked, 'Certainly?'

I told the legionnaire, 'Yes, certainly.'

I le told me that I looked a little young and that until I was seventeen, I couldn't volunteer.

I answered his statement by telling him that I was seventeen the previous month.

This seemed to satisfy him. So then he told the other sentinel to keep an eye on the gates while he took me along to see the captain.

I followed him upstairs to the first floor of the building. We passed a few legionnaires on the way. Having arrived at the captain's office, the sentinel knocked on his door and was then told to come in. So we both entered the room, and the captain asked the corporal what we wanted.

The corporal said to the captain, 'This young man wishes to volunteer for the legion and has come to find out if he can sign on.'

The captain replied, 'Thank you, corporal. Please leave us now and return to your post.'

The door closed behind him, and the captain looked directly at me and asked how old I was.

I told him that I was seventeen. Then he asked where I lived, and I told him. Beside the captain, there were two more legionnaires in the room. One of them was taking down everything I said on a paper in his own handwriting.

The other one was typing out a copy of my answers to the captain. Then I was asked if I was sure of what I was doing, because the legion, the captain explained, was very hard, and once I had signed, I would have to serve for three years. He further explained to me that after a short while in that building, with other recruits, I would be sent to Spanish territory in Africa with other legionnaires. For example, Ceuta, Larache, and Melilla. But he didn't know exactly which place I would be sent to.

After the captain had talked about the different places in Africa, it sent my imagination soaring: just like when I had been a small boy sitting, watching an adventure film in the local cinema. An excited feeling took over from a nervous one, and for a split second, I was already in Africa, wearing the uniform of the Spanish Legion.

I was brought back hastily to the present time when the captain asked me to sign the contract, if I was sure, which he had in his hand.

Before signing the document and committing myself, I asked the captain if my signing would make the three years I'd serve with the legion valid in lieu of my service with the regular Spanish Army. He assured me it would.

The papers were handed to me, with a pen, and I signed my name, with no hesitation.

After this, I was taken downstairs by a legionnaire to a dormitory where there were other new recruits. I was given some trousers and a shirt to wear, and I handed my own over, in return. My hair was then cut by the legion's barber. It was closely cropped, and I resembled a gooseberry. I was then photographed and, after that, told to join the other recruits and to select a bed for myself.

There were about twenty recruits, and I was told by one of them that we would stay there until there were ninety of us. The recruits were aged from seventeen to thirty.

By now, it was lunch time. We all sat at a large dining table, in the same room, and a legionnaire brought hot food, which was carried in a metal container for us. We had to queue up with our aluminium plate and a spoon to obtain our portion.

The meal consisted of baked beans and rice, with a piece of bread, and for those who wanted a drink of water, permission had to be given, to go outside and get it from a water tap on the patio. Every movement was watched by a guard or perhaps two of them.

Two days passed, and, in the morning of the following day, my mother arrived with one of my elder brothers. She had been very worried, not knowing where I was, and, after making enquiries to the police, was told by them to come to the recruitment legion and enquire as to whether I was there.

A legionnaire came to me and said that my mother was waiting outside, with my brother, and she wanted to speak to me. I was nervous at this prospect, as I knew it would be a shock to her when she saw me with my head shaved and wearing army clothes. However, it was something which I couldn't avoid doing, so when I went out into the street, near the main gates to speak to them, the moment my mother saw me, she started to cry.

'Why have you left us, to come to this place? I knew something was going on in your mind. You don't understand what you have done. This place is only for bad boys and bad men. Don't you realise that I can take action to get you out of this place?' My mother said.

I replied, 'No, don't do that. This is only for three years, and when I come out, I will still only be twenty. The time I serve here will count for the time I would have to serve in the regular Spanish Army.'

Then my mother said to me, 'Adventure, all you ever think about is adventure. Well, now that you've got it, where are you going from here?'

I told her, 'In a week's time we are going to Africa.'

She then said, 'All right, my son. I don't know when I'm going to see you again, but write to me as soon as you can.'

My mother then kissed me, with her eyes full of tears. Luis, my elder brother, put his arms around me and also kissed me, saying, as he did so,

'Be careful in Africa, Juan. And take care of yourself.' Then he gently led my mother away, as she was very upset and couldn't stop crying.

At that moment, I was ready to cry, myself. But then, the legionnaire, who had been watching us, came over to me and said, 'Don't worry, comrade, we're all brothers here. We all look after each other. Go and join the other recruits now and calm yourself.'

I did as he instructed, and I was very relieved that this particular episode had now passed, as it hurt me to see my mother so distressed.

A few days passed, and by this time, there were more than seventy recruits who had come from various parts of Spain. The captain came to us and told us that more recruits would be arriving the following morning, and that would make up the number required to send to Africa.

This news excited us all, and we had to prepare ourselves for moving out and very early the next morning the expected group arrived. We were then assembled into lines of six. With legionnaires placed strategically around us, all wearing guns, we were then ordered to march through the main gates, through the streets, until we arrived at the railway station where a special train was waiting for us.

We were taken in the train to Algeciras, and then we boarded a ship to 'el Puerto de Ceuta', a corner of North Africa. We were ordered by legionnaires, who were armed with guns, to get into the transport trucks, which took us to Dar Riffen, Moroccan territory, which was not yet independent.

The name of the Spanish Legion Headquarters was Don Juan de Austria, 2nd Tercio de la Legion Espanola. This was the garrison guarded by the Spanish Legionnaires. Approximately 500 men were here, defending their land.

We were then instructed to dismount from the trucks and ordered into the magazine, where we were fitted out with a complete legionnaire uniform and also given a rifle. Having completed this task, we were then shown to our dormitory, where each man selected a bed for himself and was then told by one of the corporals that we were not allowed to leave the room. We were to get a good night's sleep in order to be up early in the morning. If we needed to go to the toilet, we had to ask permission, as they were outside of the dormitory.

The next morning we were woken abruptly, by the bugler, playing reveille, and very soon the newly recruited legionnaires started to panic and dress themselves hurriedly, as there stood the corporals and sergeants, some with a belt in their hand, lashing about and shouting, 'Hurry up, you are supposed to be ready before the bugler has finished.'

We were led in formation to the canteen, where the discipline was very strict, and we were ordered to sit down, one at a time. We had to wait for the officer to arrive before we could eat. He inspected a breakfast tray and then sampled some of the food from it, and it must have been satisfactory, because afterwards, he gave the bugler the sign to play his piece of music, which was their cue, so to speak, for commencing their meal.

After breakfast, the recruits left the canteen in the same disciplined way, in silence. We marched about one mile to some fields which were private for our training. The legionnaires used this isolated spot for their practice, but the recruits came here daily to train: four hours after breakfast and two hours after lunch. The ninety recruits were divided into three groups of thirty, each group having one officer in charge, one sergeant, and four corporals.

The officer presented himself to us, and then the sergeants and the corporals, by their names. We were told that the instructions given to us, at any time, had to be obeyed. Anyone who didn't obey them would be severely punished according to the rules. The four corporals and one sergeant were to be our instructors, for the next three months.

On the final day of the third month, we had to undergo a test by the lieutenant colonel, commander-in-chief of the 2nd Tercio of the Legion. This test was to see if we were qualified sufficiently to be a 'cavalier legionnaire'.

The corporals gave us a demonstration on how to march without a rifle, and then how to march with one. The next lesson was how to change the position of the rifle from one shoulder to the other. Other various rifle positions were taught at that time. Also, how to march the correct 180 steps per minute with rifle. That was the march of the legionnaires.

We had to absorb all of this, well and truly, as in the near future, we were expected to demonstrate everything we had been shown in front of the commandant.

Some of the recruits couldn't grasp how to do the marching, so the corporal took them aside from the rest and attached a brick to each foot with some string. Then they were made to march continuously, alone, until they had got it right. Only then were they allowed to rejoin the others. And not all of us could do the runner walk properly. This was in a crouching position, looking somewhat like a frog, and at the same time, holding a heavy rifle horizontally above your shoulders.

In the heat of 100 degrees and having to keep in absolute position, going fifty yards backwards and forwards until the corporal said you could stop was no joke. Some of these recruits fell to the ground from sheer exhaustion and the corporal would then go over to the offender and kick him while telling him to get up and behave like a legionnaire, as that is what they were going to be very soon.

This runner walk was not an exercise but a punishment for failing to do the rifle movements correctly. One of the most difficult exercises was the first one we were taught, which was to smack the rifle with the flat of your right hand while holding it with the left hand before bringing it back to the right side of you while you stood to attention.

In this exercise, the cracking sound was to be heard once and that meant that every recruit did it in unison, which was difficult, and some of them failed to do.

The corporals would get very angry on these occasions, and it meant that whoever was at fault was for the high jump. The particular punishment for their error on this exercise was to be taken away from the other recruits, and facing a large, fully grown tree, they would be ordered to clout the tree twenty times with their right open hand. The corporal watching you made sure that you hit it hard each time or else, you were made to do it all over again.

I saw a recruit's hand just after he had been subjected to this punishment, and it was not a pretty sight. His hand was swollen to twice its normal size and pouring with blood. It was at this time that the corporal told us all that this was one of the legion's punishments and that if anyone complained after receiving it, their only reward would be further punishment. A double helping!

In the latter part of the afternoons, the instruction classes were held, when questions and answers were put to and required to be answered by the recruits. On these occasions, anybody who didn't know the correct answers were made to punish each other, by sitting and clouting one another across the face with the full force of their hand. This was repeated a dozen times to each man. At the end of the punishment, the face of the recruit, who was subjected to this treatment, would be swollen up and sometimes, bleeding. This was all about discipline in the legion.

The discipline and punishment which was meted out to everyone in the legion was for the purpose of turning them into real men, who would be able to cope with life in the future and come through difficulties after the strenuous training they had received in the legion.

The most important code in the Spanish Legion was, 'to me the legion', the meaning of which is that any legionnaire, away from his post, no matter where, and with or without reason, should he shout those words, any of his comrades would go to the assistance of that legionnaire in dangerous circumstances or not to defend and fight to kill, if necessary, in the defence of that legionnaire.

Many legionnaires have died through defending the honour of the Legion flag, and you can see in the museum of the Spanish Legion, all the codes inscribed in gold.

The three months' trial period for qualifying as a legionnaire was at an end the coming Saturday. Everybody was nervous, and there was tremendous tension,

I remember, as the lieutenant colonel, first chief-in-command of the Tercio, was coming to inspect us, and we were to perform all the things we had been taught during the three months, with all the other fully fledged legionnaires.

The thing we were most looking forward to was having the restrictions removed from us; for example, not being able to go to the canteen for a glass of wine with the others and fraternising with some of the special women for the legionnaires. But mostly, not being allowed to converse with the veteran legionnaires.

It was Friday, and we were taken to the magazine, where we were all fitted out with two new uniforms, hats, boots, and underwear.

The next day had arrived finally, and we were all excited. The place was a hive of activity, with legionnaires getting out for exhibition, guns of all types, from machine guns to cannons, and pistols to automatic rifles, bazookas and mortars, 51 and 81 millimetres. The legionnaires were all spruced up to look their very best and smart they looked, with their boots shining so well, you could see your face in them. They wore the green uniforms with true pride, as they had surely earned the privilege.

The legionnaires wore their shirt sleeves rolled up above their elbows, and for special occasions, they also wore round their waist, broad, black, shiny, leather belts, which was fastened with a heavy metal buckle that had the insignia of the legion engraved on it. Two more black belts were worn vertically, on these occasions, these having a smaller plain metal buckle. The hats the legionnaires wore were boat shaped and made of felt with a cord of red hanging down the right side of the wearers' face and at the end of the cord was a fringed bobble. On this important day, everyone wore the chinstrap down, which normally was kept above the hat.

The 'escuadra gastadores' consisted of ten men, who were commanded by a 1st corporal or a sergeant, and these were taller men who trained separately for the special occasions when they would march ahead of the other legionnaires. They performed rifle movements, and their signal was the striking of the ground by the corporal's rifle. They changed positions whilst marching with great precision, and a special feature of their attire was the wearing of a tool, such as an axe, shovel pick or saw, which they wore strapped to their back.

By this time, everybody was in formation, waiting for the bugler to start for the men's marching. The high-ranking military men from Ceuta and other parts of Spain were there to salute the Legion flag and the legionnaires. Relatives and visitors from far afield were also there to witness the event. The new recruits were ordered to stay behind, as we had to perform all that we had been taught in front of the colonel and others. Having done this, the colonel then told us, 'From now on, you are cavalier legionnaires. With your hat in your left hand, shout with me, 'viva Franco, viva Espana, viva La Legion.'

We did this, and afterwards, the legion band struck up the music for the march past, especially for us. We proudly paraded past all the high-ranking military men with our heads turned towards them and the Legion flag, above.

When we were told to halt by the officer, we were ordered to take the ammunition and guns back to our dormitory. The senior legionnaires returned the heavy arms to the special rooms where it was kept.

The weekend was a holiday for everybody, with full entertainment laid on, such as boxing, running, obstacle exercises, and so on, which were performed by other legionnaires, who were paid extra to exhibit these skills. Anyone who wished to do these exercises for the Saturday entertainment was invited to do so, whereby, they had to give their name to the respective officer of their company.

We had full liberty now to use the canteen and to fraternise with the women who were specially housed there for the legionnaires. Strict medical supervision and check-ups were maintained at all times. No legionnaire could indulge in sex with the women without first giving their name to the officer in charge.

This way, a high standard of hygiene ensured the legionnaire to keep a bill of good health. After intimate visits to a woman, a legionnaire had to go to the infirmary for an examination to ascertain that all was well.

Lunch time arrived, signalled by the bugler, and those who wished to eat had to get into formation and march to the canteen. Any man committing an offence, by having drunk too much wine or any troublemaking, that legionnaire would be taken away by the officer in charge. If the man resisted, he would then be removed by force, with two legionnaires holding their rifle pointed towards the offender and the officer in charge, with a pistol in his hand, telling him to walk steadily to the post guard, where he would be locked up in a cell for eight days, awaiting trial.

The punishment any such man would receive would be, from 6.30 a.m. supervised by a legionnaire and corporal, with a rifle and a pistol, to push a wheelbarrow with a shovel inside and also a hand brush and ordered to clean the grounds of the fort off any litter: the fort being approximately two miles in circumference. He would only be allowed to stop at lunchtime, twelve o'clock midday, when he would then be escorted to the canteen to collect his meal and then carry it back to the cell where he would eat it and by 1.30 p.m. would be called out again to run around the forecourt where the guards were on twenty-four-hour duty.

The unfortunate legionnaire would then be made to keep up the running in a circle, specially designed for that purpose, a hundred times. After which he would be ordered to continue the wheelbarrow task, around the fort, until six o'clock in the evening, when the flag was lowered.

This procedure was repeated for eight days; during this time, all relevant information regarding the behaviour of the legionnaire was investigated. If it was discovered that he had two previous offences, making the present one his third offence, then he would be sent to the special prison inside the fort. This was called *el peloton de los malos I*, which when translated meant, the group of bad legionnaires.

Anyone who was sent to this prison was detained there for a minimum of three months, and the punishment would be hard labour. For the whole of the three months, the legionnaire would have a sack of sand, weighing about twenty pounds, attached to his back, and every task he was ordered to do, henceforth, had to be done in a running movement. The legionnaire was never allowed to take his time or walk whilst carrying out his punishment.

It was against regulations for any other legionnaire, no matter how sympathetic, to offer a cigarette or anything else to the disgraced comrade serving out his punishment. Sometimes, off-duty legionnaires, who were relaxing and chatting outside their barracks, would see one or two or even four, sentenced legionnaires stop nearby them whilst doing their cleaning up jobs. I remember seeing a legionnaire, on one of these occasions, light up a cigarette and then throw it down on the ground so that it purposely fell close to a legionnaire who was doing punishment chores. Then after glancing quickly around him, to make certain that no guard was watching, the prisoner legionnaire furtively picked up the cigarette and, with his hand closed around it and at the same time, keeping his head low to the ground, smoked at it in a frantic fashion and nervously, as these prisoners were all searched on re-entering their cell, after each spell of punishment duty to make certain that they had nothing hidden on their person.

All the other legionnaires felt sorry for those men who were receiving such punishment, but this was the 'Spanish Legion'.

A few days later, the new legionnaires were distributed to the companies with whom they would remain for the full three years. I was sent to the fourth flag, of which there were six, in all. Each flag, or company, consisted of 120 to 180 legionnaires. All of them were fully trained commandos.

The discipline which prevailed inside the barracks was exceptionally strict, with weekly Friday inspections of everything. This included beds, uniforms, boots, belts, ammunition, and all the armaments. And on these occasions, every legionnaire had to be present and standing at the side of his bed. The only men permitted to be absent from the dormitory were the legionnaires who were on guard duty.

After the full inspection had been carried out, this being a Friday and pay day, the atmosphere relaxed a little, as everything had gone well, with no complaints and every legionnaire preparing for the following day's parade, it being Saturday.

The normal mood around the place, on a Friday evening, was happy, with the men on good behaviour, enjoying a drink in the canteen, either talking and joking amongst each other or fraternising with the women.

Even so, the legionnaires had to be present for the nightly roll-call, which took place at nine thirty regularly. After this was done, what the men did with their time, until six o'clock next morning, was their business; so long as they caused no trouble, were not caught outside of the fort, and were present and ready at the following morning's roll-call, nothing was said.

A few months passed by, and during that time, I made friends. We became more fit and proficient, as did the rest of the legionnaires who joined up, at the same time as me, from the routine of daily training and exercises. We were always improving our skills in the use of weaponry, which we practised on the adjacent beach. To the right side of the fort was a wide strip of sands and beyond these, which were about 100 yards in width, was the azure blue Mediterranean Sea, which looked so beautiful and inviting, with the sun dancing on it. The legionnaires, on their off-duty time, could go and relax on the sands if they wished. This land surrounding the fort was the exclusive property of the legion. It had been won, in some earlier battle of many years, from the Moroccans.

In the front of the fort were fields, with sparse patches of grass here and there, and it was the same around the left side and also at the back of the fort for two miles, after which the land was more desert-like.

On this particular day, three of the veteran legionnaires, who had made friends with me, and two closer friends of mine invited us to go to the beach in the evening to cool off, after the heat of the day, and to smoke a kiffi cigarette, which contained the drug that grew in the surrounding fields.

The Moroccans, who lived in the little houses two to three miles from the fort, were partly camouflaged, as the region was very hilly. They always welcomed the Spanish Legionnaires, as they spoke the language and would invite us into their humble homes, where we would sit on the floor, as there were no chairs.

The veteran legionnaires had been socialising with the Moroccans for a long time, the main reason being to purchase the drug, kiffi, as it was known, from them.

At these times, the legionnaires were always on the alert, and they had guns and knives hidden on their person, as it was not unknown for one of these Arabs, if he had drunk too much or was too high on the drug, to attack a legionnaire by wielding a stick or a knife at him. I remember on one of the few occasions that I joined them in a visit to an Arab's house to buy the drug, ten or so Moroccans were armed with huge sticks and knives, waiting outside, for us to leave the house.

It was an ugly situation and one that had to be handled with kid gloves; we had to protect ourselves, but on the other hand, we didn't want to injure any of the Arabs, as we knew that any complaint by one of them to our officers would result in an identification parade at the fort. The further consequences would mean severe punishment in the dreaded 'peloton' cell for three months or upwards.

It was three o'clock in the morning now and in the Arab's territory. So we legionnaires, though not afraid to fight, preferred, if we could, to leave their home in a peaceful way, without incident. With this our intention, two of the legionnaires went to the front door, with their hands on their gun at the ready, just in case of any attack on us by the Arabs.

We put the 'kiffi', which we had bought from them, into our pockets, and told the Arabs in the house, who had sold it to us and whom we had been talking with, to explain to the Moroccans, who were waiting outside the front of the house seemingly to make trouble with us, to leave us alone and not to make trouble because if they attacked us, we would retaliate in no uncertain way. So the friendly Arabs went out front door, ahead of us, and spoke to them in Arabic, obviously trying to placate them and warning them of our response to any aggression from them.

The angry Moroccans were shouting 'legionnaires, legionnaires' and waving their sticks and knives about in a threatening way.

Our friends told us that the thing the Moroccans wanted to fight us about was that they accused the legionnaires of going to their area for women, to have sex with. But the friendly Arabs told them that it wasn't true. The only reason we went to their homes was to purchase the drug, 'kiffi'.

Sticks and heavy stones came flying past our heads, and after this, we thought there was going to be an attack of some scale. Therefore, two of the legionnaires suggested some retaliation, as a warning. They fired a couple of shots from their pistol, into the air, with a warning that next time, it would be directly at them.

On hearing the shots ring out, the troublemakers scattered quickly, throwing the weapons they had been carrying to the ground and running for cover except for two or three of them, who had thrown themselves on the ground, with their heads bowed and their arms outstretched, begging mercy from us.

We left the Arab's house, with our guns at the ready in case of further trouble, kicking the grovelling cowards on the ground as we passed them and incidentally, who were now sympathetic towards Spanish Legionnaires, by mumbling something that sounded like 'Legionnaires, Espana', 'Legionnaires Espana'.

It was well after 3.00 a.m. now as we started to make our way home, by the light of the full moon, but we were not worried, as we had been smoking the kiffi cigarettes, which made one feel happy and carefree but a hundred per cent alert.

The reason the legionnaires smoked this drug was because it erased any unpleasant memories from the past, and it didn't impair a person's reflexes or normal thinking.

As we approached the fort, we saw a patrol of legionnaires on horseback with their officer in charge. So as not to be seen, we threw ourselves on the ground and remained in that position for about ten minutes. When the patrol was out of sight, we resumed our walk into the fort and recognised the guard on one side as being a friend of ours.

One legionnaire from the group of us spoke to him by calling his name in a whisper. The guard responded by saying, 'Who is there?'

'It's Vicente from the 4th company,' my friend replied. 'Can we come in?'

The guard answered, 'Yes, come in now, before the officer arrives.'

We sped into the barracks and made our way to the dormitory, where there was a guard on the door. This was normal procedure. He asked us for a kiffi cigarette, as he knew where we had been. We gave him a few and then went quietly to our beds to get some sleep.

The next morning, we got up and started doing our exercises for an hour, from 6.00 a.m. until 7.00 a.m. At 7.00 a.m. we had breakfast; this had to be over in thirty minutes and the canteen cleared of men. Preparation was to be completed for the usual Saturday parade, which commenced at ten o'clock and finished at ten thirty. Again, the entertainments took place until the bugler sounded that it was time for the first sitting in the canteen. This was at twelve o'clock noon. There were two more half-hourly sittings. After their lunch, the legionnaires were free to enjoy their weekend.

Some were given twenty-four-hour passes to go to Spanish territory Ceuta, the nearest city, which was about fifty miles away.

The next day, Sunday, the priest from Ceuta came to hold mass for the legionnaires who wished to attend, no matter what their particular religious persuasions. During the mass, the priest would give instructions to the bugler, not by the spoken word but by head movements, to play his bugle in a way that signified to the legionnaires which position they should be in, kneeling or standing. This applied also to the two 'gastadores', the men who led the marching procession and performed the movements with their rifle whilst doing so. All this took place out of doors, on the parade ground.

Several months passed with the same routine of training, exercising, and learning the skill of the fixed bayonet, which was required in body to body combat. In this time, I was promoted to the rank of corporal for the enthusiasm and accuracy I displayed in all of the exercises we legionnaires were put through for the Legion flag. I now had ten men under my command in combat. This entailed one mortar legionnaire, with two assistants, to feed the gun with ammunition, one machine gun, with two more assistants to refill the machine gun with ammunition, two more men for grenade throwing and automatic rifles, and a further two legionnaires, for two more automatic rifles, and myself with a pistol and an automatic 'metralleta', a small machine gun, used especially for close combat.

The following weekend, after my promotion, I was given a forty-eight-hour pass. Me and three more veteran legionnaires went to Ceuta in a transport truck and booked a bed for ourselves at the Legion Headquarters there, after which, we started to enjoy ourselves by smoking a kiffi cigarette and visiting the area of 'Jadut', which is full of Arabs and similar to the 'Casbah': a dangerous place to be in and is patrolled by the legionnaires from Ceuta and also by soldiers of the regular Spanish Army.

We went into an Arab 'cafetin' for a cup of Moroccan tea, which was served in a glass, with no milk, but mint instead. We were always careful when visiting Arab territory, knowing that our life could be in danger. There had been reports of legionnaires being killed in this particular Arab area, and it was unwise to venture around the place alone. So, as a precaution, when on a trip such as this, we took our pistol and a commando knife and kept it hidden on our person.

We were approached by an Arab, whilst sitting drinking our tea, in the cafe. He said in Spanish, 'Hello, I am a friend of the legionnaires. I served in the Spanish Regular Army. I would like you to come to my house for a drink and a smoke. I have Arab women for you, if you like, in my house. You can have sex with them if you give them a few pesetas. You can sing and enjoy yourselves, and I will cook you kebabs on the fire if you give me the money to buy the food.'

We asked him how much it was going to cost us, and he replied, 'One hundred pesetas for everything and you pay the women yourselves.'

We agreed to his proposition and went with him to his 'cavila', his home, which was about ten minutes' walk away. The humble houses were built so closely together that we had to walk one behind the other to pass between them.

On approaching the Arab's house, he stopped and told us to go inside and make ourselves comfortable. He said that he was going to talk to some Arab women called 'fatimas'. So we entered his home and looked around the place, which had no furniture of any description. There was a small carpet on the floor and a modest fireplace, which was built from a few bricks. We waited a short while, and he returned with two fatimas. We were told to sit down, and then the Arab gave instructions to one of the women to light the fire and make the tea. He spoke to her in Arabic, and she did what she was asked to do. He then sat down by the side of the fire, and one of the women then settled herself on the floor, between the Arab and one of my comrades.

The Arab then asked us if we would give him the money to buy the meat for the kebabs. We put twenty-five pesetas each and handed him the money.

The Arab then handed the money to the woman who had been waiting for the kettle to boil. She took it and left the 'cavila' to go and buy the meat. Mustafa, the Arab, then picked up a wooden box from the corner of the room and opened it in front of him, where he was now sitting. The box was full of the 'kiffi plants', from which he took several out. He closed the box and put the plants on top. Then he took hold of a knife, which he had camouflaged in his belt and started to chop up the plant very finely. At that moment, somebody knocked on the door. Mustafa told them to enter, in Arabic, and two women came into the room, wearing 'yashmaks' on their face, which left only their eyes visible.

The other legionnaires and myself then spread out around the floor, where we had been sitting, and the women then picked a legionnaire to sit down beside.

Mustafa then filled a pipe with the kiffi drug and handed it to me, as I was the closest to him. I smoked the pipe and then handed it back to him, whereupon he filled it up again with the drug and handed it this time to another legionnaire to smoke.

This was repeated until all the men had had a pipe full of the stuff. The fatima, who was sent out to buy the meat for the kebabs, returned with them, already cooked.

A glass of mint tea was handed to all of us as was a kebab on a metal skewer, and after we had eaten these, feeling happy and relaxed, we started to sing, and the women joined in.

Suddenly, the door opened, and an angry Arab rushed into the room, where we were all sitting. He had a stick in his hand and went immediately towards one of the women, apparently intending to attack her. I shouted a warning to two of my comrades, who were sitting with their back to the door and therefore weren't in a position to see the maniac enter as I was. As soon as I'd shouted 'Be careful,' the other legionnaire, who was sitting next to the woman who was going to be attacked, turned his head, spotted the intruder, and immediately lifted his foot, kicking the Arab in the stomach and making him fall to the floor, clutching himself.

We were all on our feet by this time and alert. One of the other legionnaires, who had been sitting by the door, had lifted the unwanted gate-crasher to his feet and grasping him in an unceremonious fashion, then punched him two or three times, with his clenched fist. The door was still open, and the legionnaire who had been dishing out the treatment to the Arab completed the job by taking him by the seat of his trousers and the scruff of his collar and with a running charge, threw the troublemaking Arab out of the front door.

We secured the door and after calming the women down, who were huddled in the corner of the room, frightened, stayed for a further hour or so.

Mustafa invited us to go into the small adjoining room if we wanted to have sex with the women. We took him up on his offer and went into the room, one couple at a time. They were very young women who obviously did this sort of thing, as they badly needed the money, and they knew that the legionnaires could pay them for their services. In any case, they were only treated as slaves by their Arab men.

We gave some money to the women, which was more than they expected, and some to Mustafa. In return, he gave us a handful of 'kiffi' and invited us to come again, if we wished to. We told him that we would think about it, as we didn't want the sort of trouble that had occurred earlier on. The Arab might try to get his revenge, in some way, maybe by having others with him.

Before leaving the 'cavila' Mustafa said to us, 'I would like to do some business with you legionnaires. Any time you go on holiday to Spain, remember to come and see me the day before and bring your wooden suitcase with you. I will prepare some kiffi for you and camouflage it in your case so that the customs men won't find it. Then you can sell the kiffi in Spain and make some good money for your holidays.'

We told him, 'That is a good idea. We will come and see you about it, sometime.' We then made our way into the centre of Ceuta; the time was around nine o'clock, and the sun was starting to go down, although it was comparatively light still. It was a lovely night, and we were happy, looking for further entertainment. There was plenty going on all round, bars, clubs, and so on, and plenty of women to be had, so long as you could pay for their company. The city was full of Spanish military men from the regular army, and each time we went into a bar and ordered a drink, before we could pay for it, we were informed that the drinks had already been paid for by some other soldiers from the regular army.

It seemed that the legionnaires were very popular, and everyone wanted to speak to us. The other soldiers would raise their glasses in the air, and say, 'Viva la legion. Viva la legionarios.'

It was in this bar, the third and last one we visited, that the regular army soldiers asked us to sing a legionnaires song for them, which we did. The song that we sung for them was 'The Song of the Legionnaire', and these are the words:

> I am a valiant and true Legionnaire,
>
> I am a soldier of the brave Legion,
>
> My emblem knows no fear,
>
> My destiny is only to suffer.
>
> Anyone could be anything,
>
> Nothing is important of his life in the past,
>
> All together, we support the flag of the Legion,
>
> 'Til we win or 'til we die.
>
> Legionnaire, Legionnaire, to be brave without equal.
>
> If by the shrapnel you die,
>
> You will be remembered always.
>
> Legionnaire of the National Flag.
>
> Legionnaires, go to fight,
>
> Legionnaires, go to die,
>
> Viva Espana, and viva la Legion.

It was after one o'clock in the morning when we finally arrived back at the Legion Headquarters, and we then showed our papers to the officer in charge. Having satisfied him as to who we were, we went to our dormitory, found our beds, and prepared to go to sleep.

The next day was spent pleasantly; first by finding a nice restaurant and lunching together and then going to a few bars to meet and converse with the local people, who were only too happy to chat away to us legionnaires.

By this time, our money had almost run out. So we decided to catch the truck that would take us back to Dar Riffen, where our fort was situated. We knew that the truck was scheduled to return to our barracks that evening and that it would be leaving the Legion Headquarters in Ceuta at six o'clock, so until then, we passed some time looking around at the quaint shops and bazaars, where you could buy things very cheap, and the shopkeepers were adept at haggling over prices.

One famous landmark, which could easily be seen from Ceuta's central position, was a mountain with a castle on the top, which had been turned into a prison called 'Ei Acho'. It housed only military inmates: criminals such as deserters, thieves, and men who had a record of persistent bad behaviour.

For would-be visitors, either local or tourists from mainly Spain, there were footpaths surrounded by beautifully cultivated gardens. And from the top of the mountain, by the castle prison, you could clearly see Algeciras and the rock of Gibraltar.

It was time now, to make our way back to the Legion Headquarters and to board the transport truck, which we did. The journey took about one and a half hours through dry and sandy terrain.

On our arrival back to Dar Riffen, we handed back our passes to the officer in charge and then went to the canteen to have a drink with some of our other comrades before getting ready for the ritual of the nine thirty roll-call.

Two months after this, in April, is the time in Spain of the 'Semana Santa', the saints week, when all the churches parade the saints through the streets in a procession. The 2nd Tercio of Dar Riffen sent two companies of legionnaires, in full regalia, to Ceuta. They were to march with their military band in front of the saints' procession. Not actually with them but before the religious parade started.

This was one of the important occasions in the calendar, and the streets were packed by people waiting to see the legionnaires.

Some selected legionnaires marched with their own particular saint, who was carried shoulder-high by about a 100 civilians from Ceuta. These festivities went on from eleven o'clock at night until two or even three o'clock in the morning.

When the parades and celebrations were over, the two companies of legionnaires then left Ceuta to return to the fort at Dar Riffen. Feeling exhausted, they made their way to bed; I was amongst them.

The next day was quiet, with nothing much to do, except for cleaning our rifles and other armaments. The following day we resumed our normal routine, with exercises in combat. One particular tactic we had to brush up on was how to attack a birds' nest of machine guns, which was being manned by the enemy.

This was a very dangerous mission when being carried out for real, as it entailed having to climb a hill, and once at the top of it, short of breath, and with fixed bayonets, the officer in charge would order us to throw several smoke bombs to conceal us, and at the same time, attack the enemy with the bayonet.

This was no mean task, as there were a group of enemy soldiers at each machine gun in a well camouflaged circle.

A few weeks passed by, and then it was discovered that numbers of Moroccan Arabs were standing around, outside of our fort, talking together whilst observing everything. They had camels and donkeys with them and would remain for days at a time, even erecting their tents in the surrounding fields and at close range.

The legionnaires weren't at all happy about this. There was the distinct smell of trouble. And in fact, it was the beginning of an Arab revolution against the Spanish government. They were requesting the return of their land, which we had won from them many years previously. The land which they were asking for were El Ayun, Cabo Jubi, Villacisneros, Rio de Oro, and other parts.

Our colonel gave us orders, through our officer, to go out and tell the Arabs to dismantle their tents and disperse. Also, not to come again, the way they had been doing. So two or three groups of legionnaires on horses, with their officer in command, accompanied by some legionnaires on foot, approached the Arabs and conveyed this message to them, and by force, pushing them away and breaking up their tents.

Having done this, we then returned to the fort and were immediately summoned by the bugler, signalling us to assemble. This was a general assembly, with all legionnaires on full alert and armed. Our colonel was addressing us from a platform, informing us that the Moroccan government had declared war in their territory. 'Tomorrow', he continued, 'there would be ships arriving in Ceuta from Spain, and they would be on full alert to take three flags of legionnaires of the 2nd Tercio to El Ayun.'

Company officers then gave instructions to their legionnaires to prepare the ammunition, food, medical supplies, extra clothing, and so on, for transportation on the trucks to Ceuta, which were then, in turn, to be loaded on to the waiting ships.

On the following day, we were told that the legionnaires of the 4th, 5th, 6th, and 19th flag were to board the trucks, destination Ceuta. On our arrival there, we numbered in all about 500 legionnaires. The next step in the procedure was to climb the gangplank of our respective ship.

I travelled with my company on the Gran Canarias, and the other ships were named *Almirante Cervera* and *Miguel de Cervantes*. The other ships' names evade me at the moment. What I recall vividly was the atmosphere. The legionnaires, me included, were gearing ourselves up mentally for action of the real kind.

We were at sea for two days before arriving at our destination, which was Cabo Jubi, where we disembarked to then travel by truck to El Ayun, a desert country and very hot.

At this place, which resembled an oasis, was a Spanish regular army garrison. Other companies of legionnaires were sent to other places, such as Villacisneros, Cabo Jubi, and Rio de Oro.

We quickly organised ourselves, erecting tents, our sleeping bunks, and so on and taking position on guard. We passed one or two weeks without seeing any Arabs, but then, out on patrol one day, about thirty of our group of legionnaires spotted a caravan of camels with Arabs walking through the desert, 200 yards or so away from us. There were twenty camels carrying merchandise on their backs. We approached them and stopped their caravan. Our officer then ordered us to divide ourselves into separate groups, with one half of the legionnaires to keep a look out, whilst the others checked what the merchandise which was packed on to the camels' backs contained. On inspection, rifles were discovered along with ammunition, food, tobacco, and other things.

There were two Arabs with each camel, one with a whip and the other holding on to a rope that was attached to the camel's head.

Another group of Arabs, about fifty this time, on horseback, came riding towards us, shooting at us and shouting. Immediately after seeing this, the legionnaires activated the machine guns, and opened fire on them, as the Arabs obviously meant war. Horses and Arabs went to the ground, whilst others fled to take cover. They were intimidated by our sophisticated weapons, which they couldn't match, with only rifles in their possession. Having positioned ourselves to advantage, we proceeded to pound the enemy non-stop, for around fifteen minutes with our machine gun fire. In exchange, we were receiving their rifle fire.

Realising that they couldn't win, the Arabs soon decided to throw down their inadequate weapons and sheepishly came forward, waving a white cloth, which was hoisted on top of their rifles.

The legionnaires were not to be easily conned. Knowing the cunning Arabs by this time, we held our positions without moving. Also, our officer in charge warned us to be careful, as it could be a bit of trickery by the Moroccans.

Twenty Arabs now came towards us, holding both of their hands up in the air, a gesture of genuine surrender. The frightened camels and horses were disappearing into the distance by this time. As for the Arabs, who arrived with the first caravan of camels, they were all lying face down, flat on the ground. Scattered around were the dead bodies of some Arabs and horses lying badly injured, which we had to shoot to put them out of their misery and suffering.

We had radioed for reinforcements when the firing had commenced, and now they were here. Jeeps and legionnaires on horses had come to our assistance, but by this time, the fighting was actually over, with three of our legionnaires wounded. Two of them had caught a bullet in the arm, and the other, a bullet in his leg. There were wounded men amongst the Arabs also.

Our officer in charge, ordered the wounded men to be taken to the hospital without delay. They were transported in the jeep to our military hospital at El Ayun, the wounded Arabs included, as some of these had received several bullets across the body as well as in their limbs and were bleeding profusely.

The newly arrived legionnaires on horseback were instructed to go and collect the stray animals, also the camels with the merchandise, and bring them back to where we were. Having completed this task, the Arabs were then ordered to take charge of those belonging to them respectively.

All the Spanish Legionnaires and the prisoners then walked back to the garrison at Ei Ayun. This had been one of the several similar attacks on the legionnaires in this territory.

A few months passed by, and then a complete company of legionnaires, 200 in all, set out on a reconnaissance trip in this same area. During the night, they were ambushed by more than one thousand Arabs, who killed every one of the legionnaires, including officers. It was thought that the legionnaire guards had been overpowered, under cover of darkness, before having the opportunity of giving the alarm to their sleeping comrades.

I considered myself fortunate not to have been in the company of legionnaires of that particular flag. Three days went by; none of those legionnaires returned, and it was obvious that something extraordinary was wrong.

The next morning, my company went to search for the missing men. We had walked between six to seven miles before encountering the ill-fated company of slaughtered legionnaires, all over the ground, every last one of them dead, either from mutilation or from having been shot.

After witnessing this horrible massacre, there were legionnaires in my outfit who were showing more emotion than I had previously seen. But after the sadness came a different feeling. A terrible anger swept over all of us, and what we wanted now was revenge. Legionnaires of my flag were shouting to the officers that they wanted a white card from now on. This meant licence to kill outright. Not to merely wound the enemy nor to take prisoners but to kill 'everyone'.

Our officer in charge knew exactly how we were feeling, as he was just as angry and saddened by the sight of so many brave legionnaires, no less than we were, but orders had to be obtained by General Franco and sent to us by message. No such permission of this kind was granted to the legionnaires before two weeks had elapsed.

Previous to this we had radioed to El Ayun to send twenty-five trucks so that we could bring the dead legionnaires back to the garrison. It was a very busy time, with so many funeral arrangements to be made and also, having to dig the graves in the ground which surrounded the garrison. This was a cemetery for only the legionnaires and an around-the-clock guard was kept.

At the burials, the legionnaires priest said the appropriate words and all the legionnaires presented arms, in a solemn fashion, which was kneeling on the ground, with our bayonets fixed to our rifles.

After this, we were ordered by our officer to stand to attention and replace our bayonet in its sheath, and this was followed by instructions to lift our rifle forty-five degrees skywards to give a three-shot salute as a last sign of respect to the dead legionnaires.

The officer then ordered all the legionnaires to stand to attention, and to sing, 'The Death of the Legionnaire', and these are the words:

Nobody knew in the Tercio, who was that Legionnaire.

He was so brave and fearless, he signed on in the Legion.

Nobody knew his history, but the Legion supposed he suffered great pain.

Like a wolf bite in his heart.

When someone asked about his agony, he replied with pain and sadness,

I am engaged to the dead, and I can't escape it.

I am engaged to the dead that go to unite with strong and sincere companions.

When the firing was fierce, and the fighting was hard,

Defending his flag, the Legionnaire went forward.

Without fear of the enemy's aggression, he knew how to die so bravely.

His identification recovered when they took his body from the ground,

At the end of the final battle, inside his chest, they found,

A letter and a photograph of a beautiful woman.

The letter said, 'If one day, God should call you,

To myself, I vow, that I will go in search of you.'

With his life's blood pouring on the hot ground,

The delirious Legionnaire said in a low voice,

'I am engaged to the dead, and I go to unite with my strong and
true companions.'
Legionnaires go to fight, Legionnaires go to die.

Everyone felt sad, as they returned to their respective posts, after such an occasion, and in the days and weeks that followed, many Arabs died at the hands of the Spanish Legionnaires.

By now, my service in the Spanish Legion, was coming to an end, and I was looking forward to the freedom. It was a week after this that I was summoned by my officer, who told me that I, and some other legionnaires were to prepare ourselves to go to Cabo Jubi in the early hours of the next morning. There would be a convoy of trucks leaving, and we were to go with it.

Happily, we arrived at Cabo Jubi safely, with no interference from the Arabs, and once there, we saw many reinforcements of legionnaires with weapons and arms.

We exchanged conversation with them, and whilst doing so, warned them to be on their guard at all times and not to trust the Arabs in any way.

A couple of my legionnaire friends asked the new arrivals if they had any kiffi cigarettes, as we hadn't been able to obtain any for nearly a year. We were given a packet of twenty to share between us, and we were pleased to get them.

We embarked on the ship which was to take the legionnaires back to Ceuta, but we had to wait four long hours before the ship sailed.

Two days later, we arrived at our destination and from Ceuta, we were then transferred to the trucks, with legionnaires on guard, to ensure our safe journey back to Dar Riffen.

The next day I was called to the office to sign all the papers for my demobilisation from the Spanish Legion. Having completed this, I then had to return my uniform along with everything else that was issued to me when I signed on three years previously. On the following day, I and six more men who had signed up at the same time as I had were fitted out with civilian clothing and a little money and were then escorted by legionnaires in a truck amongst others who were going to Ceuta.

When we arrived, we were given a bed, which we would require for that night, as the ship which would be taking us to Algeciras, Spain, would not be sailing until eight o'clock in the next morning.

Now though, we, seven ex-legionnaires, were free to go wherever we liked. We went into the centre of Ceuta and after having a couple of drinks in a bar, decided to go to Jadu, where my friend Mustafa lived.

We wanted to get some kiffi drug to sell, on our return to Madrid, as we had barely any money at all to start a new life. Having found Mustafa's 'cavila', his house, we knocked on the door, and it was soon opened by Mustafa himself who was surprised but glad to see me.

He invited us in and prepared a cup of mint tea for us. After drinking it, we told him what we had come for. We asked him for three pounds in weight of kiffi for four of us. The other three ex-legionnaires didn't want any, in case they would be caught with it on them by the police in Algeciras.

Mustafa said he wanted 300 pesetas from each legionnaire, so we gave the money to him, knowing that we could make a profit in the sale of the stuff.

He told us to wait while he went off to the supplier to get the drug. Not long after, he returned with a case full of the drug and then proceeded to chop it finely, as he had done on the previous occasion when he had sold us some.

We were in Mustafa's house for three hours, as it took him some time to chop such a large amount of the stuff and carefully pack into cellophane paper, which we bought at the shop for this purpose.

Having arranged it in small packs around our body, we then thanked Mustafa and left his cavila to return to Ceuta and our head quarters. We ate with the legionnaires in the canteen and had a few drinks with them before turning in for the night.

The next morning, we got ourselves ready, paying special attention to the drug which we were carrying on our body. If we were caught with the stuff, we knew for certain that it would mean a minimum of three years in prison for us.

A sergeant, with a few legionnaires drove us to the Ceuta quayside, where our ship was waiting, to pick up its passengers and cars for the two-hour journey to Algeciras. We said our goodbyes, to the other legionnaires and boarded our ship.

On our arrival at Algeciras, we had to pass through the customs, where the officers were checking everyone's luggage and belongings. We had no luggage, but we showed our military book and no questions were asked.

The train to Madrid was already in the station, and we got on it and settled ourselves in a seat. Because we had got through the customs without any difficulty, the legionnaires who were afraid to take the chance of buying kiffi were by now, very angry with themselves. However, we gave them one packet each and opened another small packet that we shared out between us to smoke on the train journey.

When we arrived at Madrid station, the three legionnaires who hadn't bought the kiffi from Mustafa said goodbye to us and went their own way but not before wishing us good luck.

The remaining four of us made our way to the district of 'Lavapies' in Madrid. On our arrival there, I went to see the woman who had done business with my ex-friend, the pickpocket, more than three years ago. She was standing in her usual place, and I approached her when she was free of other customers. I told her that my friends and I had just left the Spanish Legion and that we had some kiffi for sale and wanted to know if she was interested in buying it.

The woman seemed very surprised at my proposition but was anxious to purchase anything we had. She asked me, 'Do you have it with you now?' I told her I did, and she then invited us to her house to discuss business. We walked with her to her home, which was two or three streets away, and she invited us in. We sat down at her suggestion, and she told us that she had a son, three grown daughters, and also her husband. We met them briefly whilst we were there, and she gave us a glass of wine.

After she had examined the kiffi, we agreed on a price of 5,000 pesetas to each pound in weight. I sold her two pounds in weight and the three legionnaires with me did the same. At the end of the transaction, 10,000 pesetas was handed to each of us, and she told us not to divulge any of this to anybody. We gave her our promise that we would tell no one and that she had nothing to worry about. We took the money, thanked her, and left the house.

Once we got on to the main road again, we decided to have a last meal together. And at a very nice restaurant nearby, we had a lavish meal accompanied by some excellent wine to toast each other and our futures.

We set off in our different directions after leaving the restaurant, satisfied and happy, with the words that I'll never forget, 'viva la legion', our last exchange.

I made my way home, alone. The same as I'd been when my young dreams of adventure led me to sign on into the unknown.

I wanted to get home now, as quickly as possible, to see my mother's face wear a smile in contrast to the one of tears she wore when I last saw her. Also, I wanted to see my brothers and sister.

The taxi I called sped me quickly there and after knocking on the door, it was opened by my mother. Her surprise was tremendous, as was her joy, and although tears started again, this time, they were tears of happiness and relief, with her saying, 'My son Juan is here.' She repeated the words, with open arms, hardly believing I was really home, after such a long time.

The End

—ɯɯɷɷ◌ɛɾɵ◌◌ɾɵɷɷɯɯ—

Juan Rodriguez

THE FOREIGN LEGION

Year 1959-1965

My first three years of adventure ended with my demobilisation from the Spanish Legion. From a boy of eleven, I had started to crave for excitement from adventure films, which I used to go to see in the cinemas in Madrid, where I was born and brought up.

My father had died before I was twelve years old, after suffering an illness he contracted during the 1936-1939 Spanish Civil War. His death not only left my mother heartbroken, causing a deterioration in her own health, but also made the financial side of things even more difficult than they had been, and she had the task of bringing up single-handed, me, my four brothers, and a sister, whose ages ranged from four years to sixteen years. My only sister was the eldest, and she was being boarded and educated in a convent; this was being paid for by the nuns so that she would be able to obtain a good job in the future.

My brothers who were elder to me had to leave school around the age of twelve to go to get any sort of job they could, in the local bars or restaurants, to give my mother the money they earned to help pay for essentials. I did the same. Regarding my education, I was forced to leave school before I was eleven, as my father still needed extra money to pay for basic things, and we knew nothing of luxury, in any shape or form.

The jobs which I did were all menial, naturally. Fetching and carrying, cleaning, and all other lowly jobs that nobody else wanted to do for the few pesetas that they would be paid.

I somehow struggled through these tough and boring years, but I was forming ideas in my head about doing something constructive when I got the opportunity to seek something adventurous. So when I was seventeen, being out of work at the time, I took it upon myself, without telling anyone, not even my mother, to volunteer for the 'Spanish Legion' for three years. Details of this and what happened in those three years, I have told already, in my first adventure story.

I have now turned twenty, and I am living in my mother's house; also, my brothers are there. The house is in Madrid in an area named Estrecho.

I am newly demobilized from the Spanish Legion and looking for a job, as I have no money and have been living off the profit I made by selling the 'kiffi' drug, which I brought back from Ceuta, in Morocco, where I was stationed whilst serving my time in the Spanish Legion.

My family was supporting me financially now, and this was no good for me; either I would have to get work quickly so as to pay my way and have some money in my pocket to spend, or I must look further afield and go abroad, where opportunities would probably be better than they were here, in Madrid.

My mother was very understanding by this time, as she could see how I was feeling and realised it was difficult to obtain a job which paid a decent salary when you had no special skills.

My military service didn't help me, now that I was back in civilian life, but I kept on trying, hoping that something would turn up. It eventually did, in the shape of commis waiter work, at a hotel in the centre of Madrid.

I made a few friends whilst working there, and a girl, who was also employed at this same hotel, took a shine to me. She got very keen and wanted me to marry her. I told her that I had no savings to buy a house or anything and that

I intended to go abroad as soon as possible. She saw that there was no point in pursuing the relationship any further and things between us just stopped.

I had been at the hotel for almost a year now, and I was completely fed up, as there was no progress made in that time, and the old desire within me, for adventure, erupted again. This civilian way of life and all the monotony plus the meagre earnings were just not for me, and the itchy feet started.

I couldn't help thinking about my comrades in the Spanish Legion, now and then, and wondering what had become of them. I hadn't kept in touch with any of them, but I couldn't imagine them doing the same boring sort of work that I had done since our release from the legion.

On my next day off, I went to the government department that deals with passports. I made an application for one, giving my birth certificate, two photographs of myself, and also my military book.

It took a few days before my passport was ready to collect. During this time, I told my mother that I was planning on going abroad. To which she replied, 'This adventure business is always in your mind. You'll never settle down. I don't know how you are going to finish up, always thinking like that, with immigrating and no money or job. I don't know how you are going to survive like that.'

I said, 'what is there here in Madrid for me? Jobs with no prospects and very low wages. I have to go.'

My mother then suggested that I go to Barcelona, where her two sisters lived. 'You can stay with them, and maybe there are more job opportunities there than here, in Madrid, for you.'

I decided that when I got my wages for that week, I would leave the hotel and go to Barcelona to see if it had anything to offer me.

On my arrival in Barcelona, I made my way to the house of one of my aunts, which was in the centre of the city. I was impressed by the place, the architecture, also the flower-bedecked roads. *Paseo de las Ramblas*, a mile long boulevard, I especially remember where you can buy the best flowers in

Spain, and the merchants compete with the whole of Europe. The beautiful colourful array and the aroma of perfume you get from walking around the place are lovely.

At my aunt's, she opened the door to me, after my knocking, and had no recognition as to who I was. When I explained that I was her nephew, she showed both surprise and pleasure and invited me in.

She asked me, 'why have you come to Barcelona?' and she also wanted to know how my mother was.

I told her everybody in the family was all right and that I had come to look for a job until I had accumulated sufficient money to go abroad. Her reply to me, in that respect, was that it was going to be difficult to get work in Barcelona also, without having any skills.

'You are welcome to stay here and don't worry about paying me anything for the moment. Two of your three cousins are out of work also, as things are similar here. There is not much in the way of job vacancies', she explained to me.

The three cousins she referred to were her one daughter and two sons, whose ages were nearly the same as mine. This was my first meeting with them, and one of them had, by coincidence, just finished serving three years in the Spanish Legion, but our paths hadn't crossed, as we had been in different regiments.

We soon hit it off, and they took me for a drink, in one of the bars, not far from the house. We exchanged stories, and my cousin Elios, who had served in the Spanish Legion, was trying to help me to get a job. He showed me a hotel close by and suggested that I go the next morning to apply for work there.

The following day, the three of us went out, looking for work around the city and called in at a bar where waiters and catering staff congregated to discuss and pass on information regarding vacancies. From this source, I managed to get a part-time job. The one my cousin had suggested drew a blank.

For a few months, I did banqueting work at various hotels in Barcelona on a part-time basis, as there was nothing to be had in the way of full-time work.

Juan Rodriguez—1958 aged 22

During this spell, I registered with an employment agency in the hope that something better would turn up. It did, in the form of a full-time silver service waiter at a high-class hotel in Lausanne, Switzerland. They insisted, however, that the person who secured the position, learn their method and complete course.

I had to pay 250 pesetas to the agency, and this left me short of money, as the part-time banqueting jobs paid little. So it was after I had saved enough for my ticket to travel to Switzerland that I thanked my aunt for having me and said goodbye to my cousins, with whom I moved on, once again.

I travelled all through France and at the border changed trains for the one that would take me to Lausanne. On arrival there, I made my way to the hotel, which was situated on the side of the great lake.

At the reception desk of the hotel, I handed them the letter, which they had sent to me, confirming my position with them, and to my horror, they informed me that the job had been given to somebody else and that they had nothing to offer me.

I felt sick in the stomach and didn't know what to do. I had very little money left, after paying for the cost of the travel, expecting to be checking into a good hotel, with my bed and board taken care of, and a wage packet in return for the work, which I was looking forward to doing. Instead, I was standing here, in a strange place, unable to speak the language, with no job and nobody I knew. I felt very much alone suddenly and tired and hungry.

It appeared there was a misunderstanding between the hotel management and the agency in Barcelona, which didn't tell me that the hotel required someone immediately. I thought I could get a few pesetas together and then go, but in that time, the vacancy had been filled, and now I was in a mess.

I picked up my small attaché case and made my way out of the hotel, with my mind juggling two ideas. One idea was to make my way to Germany, and the other was to get a lift from someone who was travelling that way.

I walked back to Geneva and got on to the main road that led to the German border. I took out a piece of paper from my pocket with an address of a Spanish couple, which had been given to me by an acquaintance in Barcelona. The married couple were working in Germany at a place called Gengenbach.

After walking for an hour, whilst trying to thumb a lift, a car finally drew up at the side of me. The driver started talking to me in French, which I didn't understand. I then showed him the piece of paper I had, with the German address on it, and speaking at the same time to him in Spanish, which he didn't understand either. I kept underlining the word *Germany* on the paper with my finger. He then got the message and opened the car door, inviting me in.

I was so thankful and I was tired, as I hadn't had a meal all day. The driver of the car indicated to me that he was going to Basle. I nodded that it would be all right, and we carried on along the main road in silence. When we arrived at Basle, the car owner got out of the vehicle, and I did the same. He then explained to me, with hand movements, that the road we had travelled continued to the German border.

He shook my hand and got back in his car. I walked for about half an hour and then arrived at the German-Swiss border. Vehicles were being stopped by the German frontier police, and I carried on walking until one of them stopped me.

He asked to see my passport, and I showed it to him. He then told me to go into his office, indicating this, by pointing his finger.

Inside the office, I was instructed to sit down in a chair, which I did. I was being spoken to in German and understood nothing. Out of the four German police in the office, not one of them understood Spanish.

I had a cup of coffee that was brought to me and sat waiting for forty minutes before a different policeman was brought into the office, who then asked me questions in Spanish. He wanted to know if I was going to Germany. I told him I was. Then I was asked if I had a job to go to. I said that I didn't. The man then wanted to know if I was entering Germany as a tourist and if I had any money. I had to say no to his last question. I didn't have any money. Very quickly the policeman wrote something in my passport and stamped it. He then told me he was sorry, but I wouldn't be allowed in the country, and he then showed me out of the office, after handing me back my passport, and then he gestured to me that I go back over the border, into Swiss territory.

I made my way back to Basle, and by this time, I was feeling very hungry. It was approaching ten o'clock at night. I saw a bar lit up on the opposite side of the road and ventured across to it, hoping to buy a few sandwiches with the remaining Swiss francs I had in my pocket.

There were a mixture of ready-cut sandwiches on the counter, but I wasn't certain how many I could afford. The lady serving behind the bar was waiting for my order. I held one finger up to indicate that I wanted one sandwich, and then I held my other hand open, which contained the francs and invited her to take what the sandwich cost, from the money. She left me sufficient to buy another three, which I did. I could have eaten ten times as many; my stomach felt twisted with emptiness.

I took my sandwiches and my attaché case out of the cafe bar, and sat down on the grass verge, under a lamp post. The traffic was whizzing past in front of mesas. I hungrily ate all the sandwiches and at the same time, contemplated what to do next. I made up my mind to try again, and after spending a penny amongst the trees close by, I proceeded to get a lift to Germany, once again, with the thumb signal.

I remained in the same spot and kept waving down the oncoming cars, desperate for someone to stop. It must have been nearly an hour before a black Mercedes pulled up, and the driver got out of the car and approached me. He spoke to me in German, but I couldn't understand him. So I told him in Spanish, indicating at the same time, with my hand pointing towards the German border, 200 yards away, that I wanted to go to Germany.

He grasped my need now, and then nodding his head, he picked up my suitcase from the ground and put it in the boot of the car. He returned to where I was standing, and watching, and then he opened the back door of the car and invited me to take a seat. I was happy to do so.

Arriving at the checkpoint now, where I was previously turned away by the patrol police, I felt anxious, as if I was seen, I would be questioned again and sent back to Switzerland. So I tried to make myself invisible by shrinking myself into the upholstery of the backseat of the car.

At close inspection, the policeman who was examining the passports clearly knew the driver of the Mercedes I was travelling in, and we were waved through the barrier, with a 'gute Nacht!'

I was relieved, as I was now inside Germany. We drove along the same road for about one mile, and then the German driver stopped the car, got out, and went to the boot to get my suitcase from it.

He handed it to me, and I showed him the address I wanted to get to, on the piece of paper I had. After he saw the name Gengenbach, he indicated that I must keep on along the same road, for a good while, but that he had to branch off to the right.

We shook hands, and I said thank you to him in Spanish. I started walking, not knowing at that time that my destination was seventy miles away. I was in a strange country and with no money in my pocket. Also, I couldn't speak the language. The only thing in my favour was that it was summer time.

I had been walking for two hours along the same road in the darkness of the night, which was only broken by the amber traffic lights. I was so exhausted now that I had to find somewhere to lie down and rest. There were some large, private detached houses close by, and I saw a wooden shed in one of the gardens. I took a close look, and as it had no door on it, I went inside, but myself down in one corner of it, and went to sleep, with the thought that the next day, I would have much more walking to do.

I woke early the next morning, around 5.00 a.m. and saw that it was going to be a fine day, as the sky was a brilliant blue. I started walking towards the main road and caught sight of some apple trees. I went over to them picked one, and took a bite from it. It was lovely, and I knew that I was going to be very hungry, with no money to buy anything later on, so I picked several from the tree and put them into my suitcase before continuing my walk to Gengenbach.

I spent the next eight hours walking, only stopping occasionally to sit down at the kerb for a short rest while I ate an apple. On the way, I passed a town called Freiburg. It was one o'clock by this time, and on the opposite side of the road, a German police car pulled up. Two policemen got out of the car and came towards me. I wondered what they were going to say to me, or what they wanted me for. I was very nervous, as I thought that they were going to stop my staying in the country and put me back over the German border, into Switzerland. They started talking to me in their language, but I couldn't understand them, so then I handed my passport to one of them, and he immediately turned the pages of my passport until he came to the one which had my photograph on it and was able to establish my nationality from it. The policeman seemed satisfied with that. At any rate, he didn't notice the German stamp mark that had been put on previously, stipulating that I couldn't enter their country, as I had no money and no job to go to.

It was indeed a relief to me when I was handed my passport back, with a salute from the German policeman, instead of the complaint I was expecting to get. The two of them drove away, and I continued my walking towards Gengenbach.

By three o'clock that afternoon, it was very hot, and I had to lie down on the grass verge of the same main road, in the shade of a tree, to rest myself. At four o'clock I resumed walking and at the next junction was a signpost indicating that 'Offenbach' and 'Gengenbach' were ahead, in the direction that I was going.

It took three more hours of constant walking to bring me to the town of Offenbach. By this time, I was really struggling. The fact that I had had so little to eat, over a period of two days, was now telling on me, with the many miles in distance I had walked, also the heat to contend with.

I saw a man approaching me, and I decided to ask him how far Offenbach was from where we were. I showed him the address on my piece of paper, and after looking at it, he pointed to a built-up area, which was about 300 yards ahead of us. I got the impression from his appearance that he was a farmer, with his wellington boots and also his complexion was that of someone used to being out in the open.

I asked the stranger if he had a cigarette to give me, in Spanish. He didn't understand what I said. So then I showed him what I meant by going through the smoking motions with my hand. He got the message then and started laughing, while at the same time, taking from his back pocket, a do-it-yourself cigarette making kit. He handed me the tobacco box, which he had removed the lid from and happily gave me the papers so that I could help myself. I quickly rolled a cigarette at the invitation of this pleasant man, and after he had lit my cigarette, he walked away, with a smile on his face as he waved me farewell.

Approximately ten minutes more walking, and I arrived in the centre of the town of Offenbach. I stopped to look around for a signpost that would show me the way to Gengenbach. There were no directions to help me, so I stopped a passerby and asked him in Spanish if he could help me to get to the place that was written on my piece of paper.

The man was speaking to me in German, trying to explain. Again, I couldn't understand this foreign language. Suddenly, a small group of people had gathered round us, listening to our conversation. Nobody knew what I was saying, but it seemed that they had got the impression that I was leaving Gengenbach. However, fortunately for me, there appeared at that moment, a boy of about fourteen, who, on hearing me speaking Spanish, squeezed his way through the other people to get close to me. He asked me in Spanish what my problem was. I explained to the boy that I was making my way to Gengenbach. I also told him that I was tired and hungry, as I had been walking for two days, with practically nothing to eat, as I had no money.

The boy was both helpful and sympathetic. He said to me in my own language, 'Don't worry. My father is Spanish, and my mother is German. My father has been here for more than fifteen years. Come with me, and I will take you to the department of assistance. If they don't help you, I will take you to my father's house, and he will help you.'

I was very grateful to this boy for his spontaneous kindness and willingness to help me, a complete stranger to him. I went with him to the German government building, and we arrived there in approximately five minutes, whereupon the boy led me to a window and started talking to a woman official in German. When the two of them finished talking, the boy told me that I had to sign a paper that the woman put in front of me and then I would be given some money. I signed the official document, and she then gave me fifteen deutschmarks.

With the newly acquired money, I went to a shop nearby and bought some bread and some salami. The boy was still with me, as he was going to take me to the railway station to buy a ticket to Gengenbach. Having put me on the correct train and telling me that my destination was the next stop, we said our goodbyes, and he was gone. But not before I had thanked him for all his kindness.

The train arrived at Gengenbach in about fifteen minutes. I got off, and made my way outside the station, into the street, where I stopped a passer-by, showed him the address on my piece of paper, and made him understand that I was trying to get there.

The stranger indicated to me that the place I was looking for was the next road on the left. I walked for approximately 500 yards and came to the house I was looking for. I had no idea that it was going to be a large farmhouse, surrounded by fields, but I was very thankful to have arrived. I knocked on the front door, and a woman opened it. She was German, and when I spoke to her in Spanish, she started laughing, as she didn't understand me. Then she called someone else to come to the door, and soon, the Spanish wife of the couple who I was looking for arrived on the scene and spoke to me in my own language, which was a great relief.

She invited me inside to speak to her husband. I explained to him that one of his cousins in Barcelona, who I had previously worked with, suggested that I contact the cousin in Germany to try and get assistance from him regarding a job and a place to live until I could establish myself. That was, if the hotel in Switzerland, where I was making my way to when I left Barcelona, didn't turn out to be satisfactory. I was glad, as things turned out, that my acquaintance back in Barcelona had the idea of giving me the German contact in Gengenbach.

After I had told the Spaniard of my difficulties since arriving at the hotel in Lausanne to take up a position there and subsequently to be turned away with nothing, he very kindly invited me in and made me welcome. Before long,

I was sitting at the table with them, enjoying a hot satisfying meal, which had been cooked by the German woman, who had first opened the door to me. She was the farmer's wife, he being the owner of the three-storey house.

Jose was the name of my new friend, and his wife's name was Angelina. We were talking and having coffee after the meal, and Jose informed me that I could stay at the farmhouse and have my meals inclusive, if I wished, provided I obtained a job, for ninety Deutschmarks a month. Jose had already told me, that he was certain he could get me a job at the furniture factory where he was employed, and all this good news, which came so suddenly, left me feeling overwhelmed with relief and gratitude.

It was the German woman of the house who had told Jose, after learning of my predicament, to pass on the offer to me. She said I could have a separate bedroom and eat with everybody in the communal dining room. It was more than acceptable to me, and I was happy how things had turned out, in complete contrast to the previous two days I had spent.

The following morning, I went to the furniture factory *Uklas* at nine o'clock, where Jose was waiting for me at the factory door. He took me to the office and spoke to the manager in German. Not long after, Jose explained to me that I could start work in the factory the next day. This I did.

A few days later, Jose took me to the local police station, where I had to register as an alien working in a foreign country. I handed my passport over, and on seeing the stamp, which the border police had put on it earlier, I was asked by an officer how I managed to be in Germany when it was clear from my passport that I had been put out of the country a few days previously by the frontier police at the checkpoint.

I explained to the officer, through Jose's interpreting, that I had tried a second time to enter Germany by way of a German who had given me a lift in his car and had gone through the checkpoint, quickly, and had been waved on and saluted by the police there as if they had known one another. I stood by while Jose and the policeman exchanged conversation about my being in the country illegally. Then Jose explained to me that the aliens' officer was impressed by my perseverance and sympathetic regarding my difficulties. And because I now had a job and also a place to live, he was going to give me permission to remain and work in Germany for four years. And my passport was then stamped to that effect.

We left the police station, and I was happy and relieved, not to be thrown out of the country after all my effort to get in. Things continued in that pattern, with me working at the furniture factory, doing a very dangerous job, which entailed using a high-speed rotary saw. The repetition was soul destroying, for someone of my disposition, and after five months of doing exactly the same thing, day in and day out, the final straw for me was seeing another employee, who worked at the next bench to myself, lose all his fingers of his right hand.

I had made a few friends and had a girl since arriving in Germany, but I started to think about going to France and joining the French Foreign Legion, if they would have me. I had heard that it was very difficult to get into this renowned army, but I would have to try anyway. My three years in the Spanish Legion would carry some weight, I felt.

I duly served my notice at the factory and collected my wages. After paying the German woman of the house what I owed her for my food and board, Jose drove me to Strasbourg, the French and German border. After thanking Jose for all his help and friendship, I caught the train to Toulouse, in France. I needed money quickly, as I had almost nothing, so I started to look for a job around the restaurants and hotels. It was difficult, as nobody understood Spanish; also, with no work visa for France, I couldn't find anything.

On the second day in Toulouse, with no money or prospects of a job and no sign of assistance from anyone, I felt an urgency to get into the 'French Foreign Legion' where, at least, I would gain some dignity, having left the ranks of the unemployed.

I went to the police station, which was located in the town centre, and asked them if they could tell me where the 'French Foreign Legion' recruitment building was. I was with the police more than half an hour, trying to make myself understood, but they didn't understand Spanish, and I couldn't speak French. Finally, one of them grasped the word *legion* and two of them took me in a police car to the legion engagement centre.

I entered the main gate, where there were two legionnaires on guard. I asked one of them for direction to the right office, whereupon, the legionnaire went with me, into the adjacent building, along a corridor, and opened the door of the enlistment room. The captain in charge listened to what I had to say and soon realised that I wanted to join the legion.

He handed me an unofficial paper to read, but as it was all in French, I didn't understand it. So I handed it back to him with my passport so that it would establish my identification and other details. Also, seeing from it that I was Spanish would assist him in knowing which interpreter was required.

The captain then called a sergeant into the room. The two of them conversed a little in French, and then the sergeant started speaking to me in Spanish.

I was asked what I wanted to do, by the sergeant. I informed him that I wanted to join the French Foreign Legion. The sergeant then told me that it was very hard, that the discipline was very strict, and also that I would have to sign for a minimum of five years. He further emphasised that I should be sure of what I was letting myself in for and not regret having signed away my freedom, once the deed was done.

The sergeant then tried to clarify my reason for wishing to join the French Foreign Legion. I told him that I wished for the adventure and that I had served three years in the Spanish Legion.

He then explained this in French to the captain who was standing close by and absorbing everything that was being said.

The sergeant explained to me that I would have to sign a form now and afterwards another in Marseilles. Also, I would have to go to Paris to have my hand and fingerprints taken.

I raised no objection to any of these conditions, and so he then told me to follow him into the next room. It was a dormitory consisting of ten pairs of bunk beds, and in the room, there were several other men of different nationality, I was to discover later on. They were here as recruits, the same as myself.

One of them handed me a scrubbing brush and motioned with a circular movement that I was to scrub the floor and remove the drippings of emulsion, which was being newly applied to the wall. I was still wearing my own clothes that I came in with; no protective overalls were given to me for doing this job.

I did nothing else but remove paint from the floor for five whole days. The only relief from it was when we went to the canteen to fetch our food, which consisted of baked beans, potatoes, meat, bread, and an orange for dessert.

The following day, we were taken by truck to the railroad station, and from there we caught the train to Paris. The eight new recruits and I were guarded the whole time.

When we got to Paris, we were taken in a truck to the police headquarters to have our hand and fingerprints taken. After this, we had to go back to the station and take a different train to Marseilles. On arrival there, we were taken to the French Foreign Legion Headquarters and given a bed in a dormitory, where many other new recruits, from all parts of the world, were waiting to be posted to their eventual destinations.

Next morning, we were fitted out with legionnaires' uniforms and had our own clothes taken away, including our passports and all other personal documents that we had brought with us.

We were each given two sets of combat uniform also, a dress uniform, plus two pairs of shorts, a pair of combat boots, a pair of dress shoes, a green beret, a helmet, and a white 'kepi'. This is the unique headwear that is worn by men of the French Foreign Legion only and easily recognised by all other military units.

I remained in Marseilles for a week. We were then told to get all our personal belongings ready, as we were to be shipped out. The trucks took us to the port, and we boarded a cargo ship. Our destination was a port in northern Algeria, called Bugie, where we stayed just a few days before being taken by truck to Mascara, which was 100 miles inland from Bugie.

We noticed the change in climate. Mascara was very hot and dry. It never rained here. But at night, when the temperature dropped, it was extremely cold.

Having got over the preliminary settling in procedure, we then commenced three hard months of continuous exercises and manoeuvres, which were used in combat. This was a severe testing time, for the new recruits, and would establish which men were legionnaire materials.

I was unaware at this time that France was officially at war with Algeria, and not understanding the language kept us out of touch with what was happening in the country.

The bugler would sound reveille at six o'clock each morning, whereupon, we had to prepare ourselves, make our bed, and tidy our wardrobe, and the latter job had to be done really efficiently, with our clothes in a perfectly straight line. Shoes, boots, headwear, and so on, had to be left clean and in perfect order to be inspected, when we left our dormitory, by the officer in charge of our group, also by a sergeant and a corporal. Any complaints and the offenders' names were put on the list for everyone to see. Also, those legionnaires would have to scrub out the whole of the dormitory when they returned from a full day's training exercises.

We were allowed half an hour in the mornings to wash and dress ourselves and queue up for a drink of coffee, which we collected in our own aluminium container. This and two more pieces of aluminium formed the complete vessel, which we ate and drank from, at all times. After the drink, we had to wash the container with cold water from an outside tap. Then we had to collect our haversack, which was strapped to our back, not forgetting to pack our shovel into it, also a water bottle, and other items, as well as our rifle.

We then had to hurry downstairs to the parade ground to form groups of thirty. By this time, the corporals and sergeants would be shouting at us to move at the double.

All the trainee legionnaires then marched in formation through the main gates to the training camp, which was about two miles away. After marching for half a mile, we split into two lines and continued our march, until we arrived at our location, which was fields well isolated from inhabitants.

Once there, we were instructed to put our haversacks on the ground, in straight lines, and then to take off our combat suits and vests and put on shorts. We exercised for one hour and then got dressed again to learn the French language for one hour. After this, we learned how to march correctly: The Foreign Legion way. We did this for several hours every day. Then we had to learn how to march with our rifle.

After two hours of continuous practice, we were allowed to take a ten-minute break, for a smoke. During this relaxation period, we discovered when trying to converse with other legionnaires, which countries they came from.

Amongst the legionnaires, there were 80 per cent East and West Germans, 10 per cent French, and the remainder were made up of Russians, Czechoslovakians, Austrians, Hungarians, Italians, Chinese, and Spaniards.

It was essential to learn a common language for our communication with each other. Before long, I noticed that most of the instructors were German. They were very strict disciplinarians. Everything we did had to be exact, at all times. No man in the legion could get away with sloppiness.

Sometimes the legionnaires would march ten miles to a different training ground and stay there for three or four days. Armament skills were perfected on these trips, such as shooting with various guns, pistols, bazookas, machine guns, and grenade throwing. Real cartridges were used while training. This was so as to be able to recognise the different sounds of weapons being used.

On other days, our training concentrated on obstacles named *perqe de combat ante*; there were thirty different obstacles. This exercise had to be completed in less than five minutes.

We had to practise body to body combat, ambush tactics in darkness, and also how to survive with only tinned food in the mountains.

When we arrived back at our living headquarters, we then had a wash after cleaning all the weapons we have used, before the inspection by the officer, sergeant, and corporal. Any complaints and the legionnaires' names were entered in the officer's book for future reference and punishment.

When the three months of hard training was coming to an end, some of the would-be legionnaires had deserted. The test had proved too hard for them, as one of my friends had told me, and him being one of the deserters.

He told me, before he vanished, that he was thinking about disappearing one night, as the life was too hard and he couldn't stick it. He also suggested that I desert with him and another two that were planning to go that same night.

I told him not to get stupid ideas like that in his head as we would both be in real trouble if we got caught, and I also reminded him that there was dangerous Arab territory outside. I told him I was going to do my five years.

The next day, the three recruits in question were missing. They were nowhere to be seen around the headquarters. But it was a week after that their dead bodies were brought back by the legion. They had been killed by Arabs who worked for the French government in Algeria.

We were all shocked by the event, and it brought home to us what a deserter had to face. Had they escaped the Arabs, the Foreign Legion would never give up searching for them. It is one of the French Foreign Legion's unwritten laws. Interpol keeps a file and a photograph of all deserters.

The subject of the deserters was a taboo. The instructors and officers didn't want the other legionnaires discussing the matter, and so anyone found or heard talking about it was immediately taken away and punished.

We were told that the 'Legion', was for men and not cowards. The days seemed long because of the unending amount of exercises, the long marches, the French language we had to learn, the cleaning of the arms and weaponry, and other chores.

I was in the third section of the company, which consisted of 200 legionnaires. My German instructor sergeant put me in the front of the group when marching as he said I was good at it and set an example.

Just before the three months ended, we all had to participate in a marathon run, which was a distance of twenty miles. This was to conclude the test of stamina required by a legionnaire.

The training period finished on a Saturday, with all the legionnaires marching in full regalia, singing the legionnaires song. We marched through the city and back to our headquarters, coming to attention on the parade ground. The commandant gave a speech, complimenting us on the high marks awarded to us during the three months' training exercises.

We were now fully fledged Foreign Legionnaires, with four days completely free of all duties and three months' back pay to spend. While waiting to be posted to our destinations, we enjoyed ourselves by visiting the town centre of Mascara.

For the next few weeks, we did the full duties of the legionnaire; for example, patrolling, marching, twenty-four-hour-guard duties among other things.

On one occasion, I went with my sergeant and six more legionnaires from my section on a dangerous mission. By this time, I was in charge of my group. Other legionnaires, from another section, accompanied us on the mission. With full weapons and grenades, we marched through the surrounding streets and fields on the lookout for Arab rebels. There were reports that they had been sighted in the area, and my sergeant told me not to hesitate but shoot immediately at any approaching Arab. So we alerted ourselves, with our fingers on the trigger of our rifles or machine guns.

We entered the Arabs' houses to search for weapons and rebels, who had infiltrated civilian houses to hide themselves. They killed anyone, even their own people, if they were obstructed or not assisted by them.

In one Arab's house, we found weapons and two rebels, who were lying flat on the floor, face down, like cowards. We pushed them out into the street, keeping our rifle pointed towards them. After searching them, we found one of their flags, on each of them, was green with a white crescent moon on.

The rebels were then loaded on to a truck, and later, they were taken to our headquarters for interrogation.

By this time, the instructor sergeant, six legionnaires, and I heard shooting around us. We immediately separated ourselves into two lines, a few yards apart from each other. We then crouched behind some Arab houses, camouflaging ourselves, while at the same time, looking quickly around us to see where the firing had been coming from.

The sergeant then told me, over his special small radio, which was attached to his chest, as was mine, that if I saw any Arab carrying arms, I should shoot them without hesitation, or if they approached us, with their arms up, in surrender, to take them prisoner.

Suddenly I noticed one or two Arabs, about twenty yards away, to the right of us. I signalled with my hand to another legionnaire, who was nearest to me, to run and shoot the Arabs with his automatic rifle. I went with him, at the same time, armed with a lightweight machine gun.

By now, the Arabs had spotted us and were trying to hide themselves behind the 'cavilas', that is, Arab houses. We arrived at where they were camouflaging themselves, and we saw some of them waving their Algerian green flags. Without hesitation, I fired the machine gun at them from the corner of the cavila.

Our sergeant came with other legionnaires behind him, from round the other side of the cavila, armed with machine guns, which they pointed at the Arabs, asking them to surrender, but after they had caught sight of me, they quickly ran into an adjacent cavila in fright and refused to come out.

I called the sergeant over my radio, explaining to him that my position was good to throw a grenade into the cavila, where the Arabs were hiding. The sergeant told me to go ahead and do so.

Immediately, I threw a grenade on to the side of the cavila, not intending to kill them but to force them to come out into the open so that my sergeant could decide what to do with them.

The loud explosion from the grenade brought the Arabs running out of the cavila with their hands up and shouting, 'Don't shoot,' several times, in Arabic.

Now the other legionaries were looking around to see if there were any more 'falagas', rebel Arabs, fighting for the FLN, which is the Algerian army fighting against the French Foreign Legion and also the French Government in order to obtain their independence of Algeria.

There were many rebels scattered around all over the place and in the mountains. We took five prisoners on that occasion and some others died in the legionnaires' attack.

The commandant arrived on the scene and ordered all the legionnaires, over his radio (they were from quite a wide radius), to join together and bring the prisoners with them. We did this, and the commandant of our premier regiment ordered the whole company to walk towards our trucks, which were waiting for us.

This particular convoy consisted of twenty trucks, each carrying twenty legionnaires plus four tanks, with two legionnaires in each tank, one of them being a driver. It took four hours for the trucks to arrive at our headquarters, and the Arab prisoners were promptly locked behind bars until it was time for them to be severely interrogated by the appropriate authorities.

Some of these rebels would die, rather than disclose important information. It could take weeks to extract anything from them, and when they did speak, what they said were invariably lies. This was proven by the legionnaires acting upon their information, to us.

I was at Mascara for about six months, doing reconnaissance with other legionnaires, around the mountains, in search of rebels and also to get fit for action, at any time.

Shortly after this, I was called by the commandant of my company to his office. Whereupon, I knocked at his door and presented myself in the correct and only acceptable manner.

First, I gave my name. Then, I informed that I was from the fourth company of the premier regiment etrangere. After that, I had to give my matricula accompanied by my special number, proving who I was. Whilst giving my commandant this information, I stood in front of him, to attention, dressed in my best brown uniform and holding my white 'kepi' (hat) in my left hand, at the side of me.

When I had completed my presentation to the commandant, he told me, 'Legionnaire Rodriguez, after studying your reports, which have been brought to my attention by your instructor officer and sergeants, I notice that you have always received top marks in your four months of exercise training. Therefore, I am happy to inform you that you now qualify for a promotion and to have more advanced courses. The ones which are open to you are the corporal's course, the parachute course, or the telegraphic in radio and communications. Personally, I feel you must specialise in Morse code and radio operator work, and the legion is in need of these particular specialists.' He went on, 'Your understanding of the French language is good and with your high examination marks in radio Morse code, as well, I have decided to send you tomorrow to the headquarters of Sidi-Bel Abbes to commence a course lasting four months as a radio telegraphic.'

After listening to everything my commandant had to say to me, he then handed me a certificate of entry into the above stated course, and I was dismissed.

On returning to my sergeant in order to explain my departure from the unit, he informed me that he was already aware of my posting to Sidi-Bel Abbes the following day, as he had previously discussed the matter of my promotion with the commandant.

On the way back to my dormitory, I was feeling pleasantly surprised and also looking forward to the new adventure.

Other legionnaires who had completed the extremely disciplined four months' training period, I learned at that time, were being sent to other regiments which were situated all over Algeria.

These other regiments included the premier, the second, the third, the fourth, plus the special unit, which was the 13th Demi-brigade of the legion etrangere.

Each regiment of five companies had, within them, one company devoted to the control of ammunition, food, telecommunications, doctors and medicine, and all dead personnel—both legionnaires and Arab rebels. The men of the other companies were for 'action'.

All companies were divided into five sections, and the total number of legionnaires was between 12,000 and 16,000, all ready for action.

Next day, I and many other legionnaires were transported by a convoy of trucks and tanks to Sidi-Bel Abbes. The journey took approximately six hours over uninhabited desert-like land, which was surrounded by high mountains, and the climate was very hot.

Every legionnaire carried his own equipment in his backpack, which was strapped across his back, and also his automatic rifle, or machine gun, plus his ammunition.

On arrival at Sidi-Bel Abbes, I then presented myself to the officer in charge at the headquarters of the premier regiment etrangere, whereupon,

I and another legionnaire, who was sent to accompany me, went to my dormitory, where I was shown my bed and wardrobe. This was to be my home for the next four months. I then made up my bed, unpacked my personal things, and put them tidily in their appropriate place.

I then noticed other legionnaires in the dormitory, some sitting relaxing on their beds and others sitting at a table in the centre of the room, which was for the personal use of the legionnaires billeted in that dormitory.

They had come to do the same course as myself, which commenced the following day, after a formal presentation to the instructors.

At seven o'clock next morning, four groups of legionnaires, twenty-four in each group, assembled on the parade ground in front of the barracks. This building was for the express purpose of specialty training courses, and only legionnaires sent to study a particular course were allowed on the premises.

These legionnaires were exempted from all other duties, such as hunting Arab rebels, guard duties, and so on, and spent each full day, with the exception of Sundays, studying the specialised course, for which they had been assigned. Their working day finished at the lowering of the flag, which was at six o'clock in the evening.

The lunch break was taken from twelve thirty in the afternoon until two o'clock. In the barracks' canteen, the discipline remained, with strict formation of the legionnaires to collect their food and take it back to their table.

This was presided over by three sergeants and one officer. The meal consisted of soup, fried eggs, potatoes or meat, and baked beans. Dessert would be a milky rice pudding or an orange. Drinks available were either water or wine.

My course instructors were one brigadier, two sergeants, plus a captain who were French. The others who taught me radio Morse-code telecommunications were German.

The nationality of my comrades who were also taking this course were twelve Germans, ten Frenchmen, one Italian, and myself, a Spaniard.

Our day began at seven o'clock in the morning, and the first hour before study was taken up by exercises to keep us fit. They entailed running and various physical movements.

At eight o'clock, our study instructors would be waiting to take us to a special room, which was equipped with the appropriate apparatus. There were twenty-four tables in the room: one legionnaire to each table, with headphones, a manipulator, exam papers, and pens for writing.

All conversation was in French, and it was strictly forbidden to use any other language.

We were taught the American method, which was G.R.C.9 American radio, long and short frequency, from which we could receive messages and send them, as far as 600 miles away, with the appropriate antenna, and this was the particular apparatus, which we took into the mountains withies. It worked on both battery and electricity.

The course was difficult, which made the days seem long. We would have weekly tests, each Friday, to see who was progressing and who was not.

At the end of the four months' course, I passed the 151 and the 251 courses, but, out of the twenty-four legionnaires to enter, there were six failures, who were made to continue for another two months, or else they would be sent to join the action company.

On Sunday evenings, six to eight legionnaires would go into the city of Sidi-Bel Abbes for a drink in the bars when we always had to be on our guard, as the Arabs felt distinctly hostile towards us while at the same time nervous, and their expression of suspicion didn't escape us.

When the four months' radio-telecommunications course ended, I was presented to my commandant to receive the certificate and a commendation. This included being praised for attaining high marks in the 151 and 251 courses and also for learning the French language.

I was posted to the second regiment, fourth company, two days after and joined a convoy of twelve trucks and eight tanks. I was in the jeep that was leading the convoy, and my commandant was in the front of the same jeep. I was in charge of the radio to send and receive messages to other sections of our company.

It was seven o'clock in the morning that our convoy headed towards the mountains and after travelling for about six hours, everybody got out of their vehicle and with their pack on their back and carrying their weapon and ammunition, walked up into the mountains, looking for Arab rebels, who were hiding in scattered groups.

The legionnaires divided into groups so as to cover mare ground, and I had to keep close to the commandant in order to give and receive radio messages to legionnaires of the other sections.

After one or two hours of dangerous mountain climbing, we reached a peak from where we could look down on to lower flat shelves and shrubbery that grew amidst the rocks.

It was not long after that we heard machine gun fire. Not knowing where it came from, all the legionnaires automatically dropped to the ground whilst seeking to camouflage themselves.

My commandant, who was in a crouching position at the side of me, urgently requested that I hand him the telephone from my radio, which I did.

He spoke to the officer of the first section, wishing to know if he had any knowledge of where the machine gun fire was coming from. The radio officer informed the commandant that his section had located two machine guns which were 200 metres to the right of us. The commandant then told the officer, over the radio, that we would advance in an effort to capture the Arabs, who were manning the machine guns.

Our commandant then stood up, and, with both arms outstretched, gave the signal for all the legionnaires to advance.

It was around three o'clock in the afternoon; by this time, the sun was high, putting the temperature in the nineties. The perspiration was pouring from my face, and the equipment on my back weighed heavy. As I caught sight of my commandant, who kept just ahead of me, I noticed that his combat jacket was soaked in sweat, even though he carried nothing on his back, as did the other legionnaires.

Water was precious and more so because sometimes on these rebel-hunting operations, it could be two days without contact of the provision carrying convoy trucks.

At this particular time, we were caught up in intense firing from the Arabs, and the bullets were screaming past my head. After an hour of rapid exchange of shooting between the Arab rebels and ourselves, we pressurised them and caught them in an ambush. This tactic had been planned by the commandant, and it paid off because immediately afterwards, the rebels came out of the hiding, holding a white flag in surrender. We saw that some of them had their green national flag wrapped around their bodies.

We took twelve prisoners along with their armaments of machine guns, automatic rifles, hand grenades, plus dynamite, and some of them were carrying maps of Algeria.

Having put them under heavy guard, our legionnaires toured the vicinity and discovered twenty dead Arab rebels. There were no legionnaires killed on that occasion, just three slightly injured.

Messages from the other sections of our company were coming through to me, via my radio, which I passed to the commandant.

We stopped for a break after this violent attack, and we were instructed to eat. Our meal consisted of baked beans and cold tinned meat, which we carried in our kit bags. One or two legionnaires built a fire and made coffee with some of the water we had in the round canteen strapped to our body.

When we had finished the meal and rested ourselves, which lasted for an hour, the commandant requested me to transmit a message, which he had written down on a piece of paper and had handed to me. This message was to inform the convoy to head towards a sector near to the foot of the mountains where we were heading ourselves.

We made our way down the mountains, a slow descent, of three to four miles and joined the convoy of trucks and tanks which we then boarded to make our journey back to the headquarters. All the legionnaires, including myself were very tired. We were pleased to see our vehicles. My radio assistant and I rode back in the same jeep as the commandant and his special assistant.

After travelling for about five hours, through open fields, we finally reached our headquarters. We dismounted, and everyone returned to their dormitory.

One of the sergeants told a legionnaire to bring water in a canister from the water-tank truck, which was kept outside the building. Another legionnaire distributed it to each man, in turn, as they queued up with their helmet for their share. They then washed themselves in an adjacent room to the dormitory, which was mostly empty except for two tables, which the legionnaires ate from. The canteen was then opened up and the men were at liberty to relax and buy beer, snacks (which were only packets of biscuits), and cigarettes.

The building that was our headquarters was situated in the desert, at a place called *El Salen*. It was fifty miles to the nearest inhabitants.

When the fuel for the generator ran out, we had to manage with just hand torches until a new supply of fuel reached us. The same applied to the food. We would be on short rations, with no bread, potatoes, or eggs, just tinned food. There weren't any proper cooks anyway and no proper kitchen.

Next morning, I was called by the commandant to his office. After I presented myself in the correct way, he informed me that I was to remain in that combat company for the rest of my five-year contract with the French Foreign Legion. He went on to explain that I had been designated to the fourth company of the second regiment to act as his personal radio operator, and I had to work and liaise with the other four sections of 'the fourth company'. The commandant also told me that I would have to work on the radio in his jeep, on operations when necessary, and at other times in the barracks, in a special room adapted for long-distance telecommunications, which had an appropriate powerful generator and battery working in coordination with the antenna, and radio G.R.C.9.

I was then ordered to present myself to the radio officer, also the radio sergeant, and four radio-operator legionnaires. Following this, I had to return to my dormitory to clean my weapons and check my cartridges and grenades in readiness for the next spell of action. All legionnaires had to be on alert, all the times, around the clock.

My guard duty time was to be spent at the radio controls, and the rest of the time, practising code deciphering.

We passed two days like this, and then I got a message through radio from the headquarters, telling us to go out on reconnaissance to *Reggan*, *Atn Salah* and *Ahaggar* mountains, where many 'falagas', Arab rebels, had been sighted. We were to join other companies from other regiments, both legionnaires and the French troops.

I gave the message to the commandant, who, in turn, passed the message on to his officers, who ordered us to prepare ourselves and be ready to leave in half an hour with sufficient food for five days, also, water and sleeping bags, and 500 cartridges of ammunition per legionnaire.

At twelve midnight, the men boarded the convoy of trucks and tanks. The radio jeeps were spaced between at intervals, and the tanks were both in the front and the back of the trucks.

After fifty kilometres on the road, the commandant stopped the convoy and gave orders through the radio to the other sections of legionnaires to continue with caution, as the rebels were known to be scattered in the area. The darkness was broken only by the moonlight.

I was close to the commandant, a sergeant, and five other legionnaires. We continued through the fields for another hour when suddenly the burst of machine gun fire ended the silence, and grenades thrown by the enemy were exploding in front of us. The commandant then gave orders to the other sections to encircle the Arab rebels without shooting, and another company, a few miles away were ordered to keep a watch out for rebels retreating from the ambush of the fourth company.

The shooting stopped, and all was calm again. The legionnaires covered another 500 metres of ground to ensure that there were no more rebels. The commandant gave the order for everyone to return to the convoy of the trucks which was to form in a circle, a 100 metres in width.

We were to settle down for the night, and any legionnaire wishing to make a fire could do so. With branches from the bushes that grew wild in the fields, we built a fire and boiled some water to make coffee. Afterwards, we unrolled our sleeping bags, and the sergeants arranged the guard duties around the camp. Some legionnaires sat talking around the firelight for an hour.

I was in radio contact with other companies within a radius of five miles, checking that everything was all right and that there was no sign of rebels around. I passed the message to the other radio sections that I had done my two hours radio contact and that they were in charge from then on.

I slept until five in the morning and saw the sun rising. The commandant was already getting ready himself. He told me to call the other sections over the radio and order them to prepare themselves after they had drunk their morning coffee and to walk in a semicircle up the mountains, in search of Arab rebels.

After about two miles of walking, we found ourselves in the firing line of the enemy again. The other legionnaires and I immediately dropped to the ground and retaliated by firing back at them.

The legionnaires using rifles were accurate marksmen at a distance of 200 metres, as was I, but at this particular time, I was using a small machine gun called a 'metralleta' which hits its target at ten to twenty metres.

Our company endured intense fire from the Arab rebels for about fifteen minutes until grenades and rockets from another section of legionnaires overwhelmed them, and when the firing stopped, the rebels were found to be dead.

We dug a grave and buried the ten or twelve 'falagas', after which we continued for two more days in search of these rebels, but there were no more to be seen.

The supply of food and water we brought with us was almost gone, so we returned to our convoy of trucks, which we located through the radio and made the four- to five-hour journey back to the headquarters.

The routine was the same: taking water to the dormitory to wash and shave and after cleaning the weapons, have a meal of tinned food. The legionnaires could then relax, talking and buying beer if they wished from a small canteen, which was in fact just a small room, opened specifically for men to buy beer and cigarettes.

After almost a year in this place, *El Salen*, we continued operations in the fields and mountains; Algeria was reaching near the time of independence.

I received a message through my radio in Morse-code, saying that we had to leave immediately, taking all the armaments, ammunition, and food with us.

After destroying the camp, by blowing it up, the message continued, in ZBO, vacate the area and make your way to the capital, Algiers, where an army of falagas is approaching.

It was early the following morning that the legionnaires, having prepared everything, left in a convoy of twenty-five trucks, six tanks, and six jeeps, for Algiers.

There were 500 of us, and on approaching the suburbs of the capital, the legionnaires dismounted from the trucks except for fifty men, who were left to guard the vehicles and two tanks.

Our commandant gave orders to the whole company to march in two lines, until we arrived at the city. Once in the city, we divided into groups of ten. By this time, we could hear machine gun fire, and grenades exploding. The parachute regiment of legionnaires were already engaged in heavy fighting with the falagas, who were hiding in some of the buildings in the capital.

We made our way through the roads, searching the buildings and taking possession, forcing the Arab rebels out into the streets for interrogation. Whilst doing this, we were being shot at by rebels who had positioned themselves in the windows of some of the houses.

Fierce fighting continued in Algiers for six hours non-stop, with many casualties of falagas and a few legionnaires killed, from both the parachute regiment and also our company.

After handing the prisoners over to the French regiment, who were on standby about a mile away, the legionnaires then pulled out of Algiers, and my company returned to the convoy of the trucks, where we remained for two days just in case things flared up again.

As things had calmed down between the Arabs and the FLN rebels, the legionnaires left the place and headed towards *Oran*, taking up residence in a deserted barracks, where we stayed for a month and awaiting orders from our headquarters as to the time of independence of Algeria.

The FLN was the new government of Algeria, and they installed their own army.

One day in the following week, we were back in Algiers, where we stationed ourselves around the streets with our trucks. We were on full guard, in case of trouble or an attack on us.

Things stayed calm, so the legionnaires moved on to the port of Algiers, in barracks, on standby. The legion was requesting volunteers for Madagascar, Tahiti, and Djibouti. I volunteered to go to Djibouti: a French port situated near Ethiopia, the Gulf of Aden, central East Africa, and the Somali Republic Françoise.

The journey to Djibouti by ship took eight days, with one stop in Egypt. Our new uniform for the very hot climate was of a cream coloured lightweight material, with shorts replacing full length trousers and short-sleeved shirts.

On arrival, we were transported by a truck to the headquarters of Djibouti, where we remained for two days. We prepared ourselves with all the necessary equipment, including tent-making material and camp beds and also, food, weapons, and ammunition.

We went by special train to a place called *Holhol*, which was about thirty-five miles from Djibouti. It was the only train making the journey to the frontier of Ethiopia, approximately fifty kilometres away from *Holhol*.

The destination of the third company of legionnaires was near to Addis Ababa. My company, the fourth company, was stationed at *Holhol*, whilst the first and second companies were stationed on a small island off Djibouti.

In the beginning of my two-and-a-half-year stay, we slept in tents and ate from our metal food container. The climate here was something extraordinary for us to adapt to. We had to take daily doses of quinine to protect us from contracting malaria and typhoid and to withstand the intolerable heat.

The temperature rose to forty to forty-six degrees from one o'clock to three o'clock in the afternoon, and some legionnaires would faint.

Our day commenced at seven o'clock in the mornings, with an hour spent doing physical exercises. Then we erected showers, and obtained water from ten kilometres away. The Somalis had made a small reservoir and fitted pipes to enable the water to be pumped through to the village, where about 500 Somalis were living.

We would spend eight hours a day, building a barracks with cement and bricks. This had an outside wall, a metre high. The sweat poured off us, as we used a pickaxe to level the ground. Boulders had to be removed from the foundations and carted away over the cliffs. This, and all the shovelling, was heavy work.

For two hours, when the sun was at its hottest, the legionnaires were allowed to relax or sleep inside their tents. But it was still too uncomfortably hot and stifling, with no breeze.

We finished work at five thirty in the evening, and had a wash and brush up before eating. Sometimes there was no water to wash with. At times like these, a group of eight legionnaires would have to go to the reservoir and ask the Somalis why the water wasn't coming through the pipes. They would reply that there was a blockage of soil, which was preventing the water coming through. The legionnaires would have to shovel soil away until the water pump started working again.

It was six months later that we vacated the tents to move into the newly built barracks. We were given new blue uniforms, and our next task was to build a road to enable trucks to reach us. The road was half a mile long from the railway station in the village to the new camp. It took us three months to complete the road.

The Somali Republic Françoise was a French colony, and the legionnaires' purpose was to keep peace in Somalia and Djibouti and keep the Ethiopians and Mogadishus out, thus preventing the French port of Djibouti from being overtaken.

The heat in Djibouti was forty degrees at one o'clock in the afternoon and water was very scarce, with practically no rainfall. Ships from many parts of the world would drop anchor here, bringing different cargoes.

The legionnaires were very happy, having completed the building of the barracks and the road. They were then told by the commandant that they could have a forty-eight-hour pass to go into Djibouti. Our wages had accumulated, through lack of opportunity to spend it, but now they were free to do so.

Turns had to be taken, with thirty legionnaires off duty at a time. It was one month before I was able to go to Djibouti for forty-eight hours. I went in my best cream uniform and white kepi, also the yellow lance of honour which was awarded to my regiment for its time in combat in Algeria and other parts of the world.

The legionnaires, who went on that occasion with me, split up going their different ways to enjoy themselves. One other legionnaire and I stayed together.

We went to a bar for a drink, where everyone welcomed us and bought us drinks. Afterwards, we went to a good restaurant for a slap-up meal and then walked through the Somali area, where the houses were of very low standard, made from sand and bamboo.

Women started calling us with open hands, asking for money. It was outside of their houses that they were telling us that they hadn't eaten, with hand gestures to their stomachs and mouths.

We gave them a few francs and continued walking along the dry, dusty road, where a woman standing at her front door called 'Legionnaire, Legionnaire', whereupon, I turned around and saw a very old woman. My comrade had already gone with the first woman, who was young, into her house.

I felt sorry for the old woman and approached her, wondering what she was going to say. She spoke in broken French, asking me if I had a cigarette for her. I gave her one and then lit it for her. She invited me into her house. I was curious as she was very old and her face had wrinkles.

She told me that she was 104 years old, also that her family didn't help her or give her any food, and that she was hungry. I noticed that she was all bones, with very little flesh on her. She was friendly and wanted to make tea for me. She was explaining that her family lived in the adjacent houses.

I felt pity for the poor old woman and gave her 500 francs. She was very pleased and motioned with her hand that she wished me to stay, while she called one of her relatives in her native Somali language.

I still remained standing, just inside the room, which had no furniture, just some floor covering made from woven bamboo. There was a small fire burning in the middle of the room. This was their means of cooking and boiling water.

Three women appeared and looked surprised to see me there. They said, 'Hello, Legionnaire,' in French, to me, and the old woman went on to explain that one of the women was her daughter; the others being her granddaughter and her great-granddaughter. There were no men to be seen around the place.

One of the women boiled some water in a small round metal vessel and made tea. It was herbal, and she handed me a glass. I sat down on a piece of wood that had been cut from a tree at the side of the room. The old woman threw something on the fire, which gave off a strong aromatic smell, like incense. They were possibly incense sticks.

The walls were painted in different colours, figures, and shapes, and the old woman started praying to them and doing some arm movements while at the same time mumbling in Somali.

I asked her why she did that and she told me that she had put the bad spirits out of the room and prayed to the good spirits on the wall. Afterwards, she came over to me and said that she was praying that I would always have good spirits around me.

One of the other women had been asked to get some chicken by the old lady. The old lady had given her some money from the money that I had given her. The woman returned with live chickens, which were killed in the next room; then they prepared and cooked. I was invited to eat with them which I duly obliged. The chicken was offered to me from a primitive frying pan, and I took a piece and ate it with my fingers—the same way as the others did.

I was there for about three hours; then I told the old woman that it was time for me to leave. She wished to give me a present by offering the services of her granddaughter, which I declined. I then left.

I made my way back to the town and looked in at some of the bars, where I caught up with a few of the legionnaires from my company. We drank and chatted, had a meal, and got into company with women who were working there for the pleasure of men.

When the pass expired, I made my way back by train to *Holhol*. Some of the legionnaires were found to be drunk on their return to camp and were promptly put in prison by the officer in charge. They were found to be unfit to take up their duties. The discipline of the legion was always severe.

A few weeks later, some twenty legionnaires, including myself were ordered to go and pick up 400 Somali prisoners from the railway station at Djibouti. They were passed on to us from the Somali and French governments. They were thieves, rebels, and criminals, and we put them in big tents, 400 metres away from our own camp. They were surrounded by barbed wire, which we connected to live electric cables and a twenty-four-hour guard was posted for security.

These prisoners were sent to us specifically to build a road from *Holhol* to Djibouti and so the next morning, we took most of them in trucks, with all the necessary tools for the job, including dynamite.

The legionnaires guarding them were given orders to shoot to kill any prisoners trying to escape during the project. Our interpreters told them this in their own Somali language so that they understood.

The making of the road was hot and heavy work, as the ground had to be opened dug up with a pickaxe so that the boulders and large stones could be removed before levelling, and then the gravel and sand spread on a smooth surface of small stones, which had been previously laid.

The work started every morning at eight o'clock until one o'clock and continued from three o'clock until five o'clock in the evening, with only Sundays being days off. Relaxation was inside the prison.

A few of these men did try to escape, and they were shot and killed by the legionnaires who were supervising them.

Standing all these hours under the blazing sun was intolerable. But this was the Foreign Legion and everyone in it had volunteered their life to it for five years, so there was no point in complaining.

A complaint to your officer got you eight days in prison. Only when a legionnaire fainted did he receive any assistance. On such an occasion, he would immediately be taken to the infirmary by a jeep, a truck, or helicopter, depending on the distance from the camp. If the latter was required, it would be requested via radio.

During this time, we had early morning exercises, which commenced at six thirty and at seven thirty, we stopped for a coffee break. After this, we prepared ourselves for duty.

We had two marches of thirty miles every week. Two or three legionnaires would faint to the ground from heat exhaustion and insufficient water. They would then be given injections to revive them.

Proper cooks and a fully equipped kitchen were amongst the improvements at our newly built barracks. A canteen was available with table and chairs to eat properly, including cutlery and also glasses to drink wine or water from. Fresh bread and plenty of food was available.

A bordello, especially for the legionnaires was situated about fifty-five yards outside of the camp. Twenty women from France and Djibouti were employed by the Foreign Legion and were medically checked all the time, as were the legionnaires.

At Holhol, with me were men of German nationality along with Russians, Hungarians, Czechoslovakians, Chinese, French, Italians, Polish, and Spanish. These were my comrades, who I was working with every day. Frequently, I listened to the conversations about politics with the Germans mentioning 'Hitler' during World War II.

I made friends with my sergeants and brigadiers. One of them told me that he had been a member of the SS, working for Hitler. To confirm this, he showed me photographs of himself when he was in the Gestapo in the company of Hitler and wearing the uniform with the SS emblem.

After the defeat of Germany, many of them had fled to France and joined the Foreign Legion under an assumed name. It was noticeable that they were hard, extremely disciplined characters, and highly intelligent.

Some weeks later, we had to dress in full regalia and go to Djibouti by train to do a march past for an inspection in front of a general, who had been sent by General De Gaulle.

The legionnaires enjoyed these occasions because after the ceremony, they were free for the rest of the day to do as they liked, as long as they returned to Holhol by special train early the following morning.

Two weeks later, it was discovered that four legionnaires had deserted. A French sea patrol brought back two of them, who were on a boat that they had stolen with the intention of getting away to southern Yemen. The other two died in a shootout while resisting arrest by the patrol legionnaires, who were being fired at by the offenders.

The two who were brought back to our company were made to serve hard labour every day for an indefinite period. This entailed the breaking of stones with a large hammer commencing from six thirty in the morning until darkness fell and only stopping for meals.

They were guarded by a sergeant with a gun and two legionnaires with rifles. The punishment was halted after a month by the commandant. He then had the two prisoners sent to a French detention prison to be sentenced by a military court and to continue their punishment, even after their five years' term had expired.

One particular week, we went on operations of contraband goods, such as cameras, watches, drugs, and arms, which were smuggled aboard camels from Somali and Ethiopia into Djibouti.

We stopped a caravan of twelve camels in the middle of the desert. After searching them, we found cameras, watches, and marijuana. We confiscated the things and took the Somalis prisoners, later returning them to the authorities.

My section of the fourth company of the second regiment was given a month's holiday on a deserted island off Djibouti. The only occupants were two companies of the Foreign Legion. They were the first and the second company to guard the island. We made the journey by air. On arrival there, we discovered that it was even hotter than Djibouti. Everything was bleached white by the sun. And the sand, which was too hot for bare feet, was like fine, white salt.

At night we used to go to the beach, quietly watching the giant turtles that came in from the sea to dig holes in the sand, where they laid their eggs. The fish were of brilliant tropical colours and while swimming under the water, wearing goggles and flippers, we could see shoals of them. But there were sharks also in these waters, so we had to take care.

This was the month of July and at the end of the holiday, we returned to Djibouti and then to Holhol by train where we remained for a further two and a half months.

I and five other legionnaires were then sent back once more to Djibouti and after two weeks there, we travelled to Marseilles by ship. There were twenty legionnaires by now and on arrival at Marseilles, we went to the headquarters where our legal documents stating that we had completed our five years in the legion were being finalised.

We stayed in Marseilles for a month without any duties. We didn't even have to get up early in the mornings, but when we wanted to, we could go into the town as we wished.

One day in the following week, I received all my papers with passport and back pay, accompanied by a train ticket to Madrid, in Spain, and I was also fitted out with new clothes and shoes.

The commandant told me that if I wanted to re-engage for three more years in the Foreign Legion, I would have to be back there before forty days, and that way, I wouldn't lose any privileges with the legion.

I said, 'Thank you very much,' and after saluting him and shaking his hand, I turned and left. As I came through the main entrance door of the headquarters, I saw two legionnaires on guard, and as I passed them, I said, 'Au revoir Legionnaire' with a last salute.

The End

This is the second story of my adventures, and the third is my experience as a mercenary, working for President General Mobutu in the Belgian Congo, now Zaire.

Juan Rodriguez

'THE CONGO'

Where Men Are Eaten

An authentic account of my year in the
Belgian Congo: 1965-1966

Written by

Juan A Rodriguez

Having completed five years service in the French Foreign Legion, I travelled immediately to Madrid, in Spain, from Marseilles to see my mother, sister, and brothers, whom I hadn't seen in all that time.

I was feeling nervous, as I had been out of touch with the civilian way of life for what seemed like a very long time. But on the other hand, I was happy to be free from the French Foreign Legion and still alive after the close encounters I had experienced in the war in Algeria.

The hard discipline of the French Foreign Legion and the memory of the dead legionnaires who had been my comrades left a feeling of sadness and resentfulness inside me.

I had little money, and so familiar thoughts of obtaining work were going around in my head as I took a taxi from Madrid railway station to my mother's fourth storey flat in the suburbs. Once there, I rung the bell and waited for the door to be opened.

My mother soon appeared in front of me and after a slight hesitation, while she studied me, she recognised her adventurous son, who was, by now, very brown from the burning sun of Djibouti.

A smile spread over her face, and she then started to cry, at the same time. 'Oh my son, Juan, you're still alive! I had thought many times that you would be killed, and I would never see you again,' she said. She put her arms around me, and I consoled her by telling her not to cry, as I was alive. I saw my sister and young brother, who were at home from work for their lunch break. By the end of the day, I was very tired from unending questions about my experiences.

I gave my mother some money for my board and on the following day, I went to the centre of Madrid to look for work but without success.

To pass the time, I went to look up some of my old friends, who were pleased to see me and surprised to learn that I had served five years in the French Foreign Legion. They were curious and suggested going for a drink in a bar. They insisted on paying while they questioned me unceasingly about my experiences. They wanted to know how to volunteer for the Foreign Legion compared to their somewhat tame existence in civilian life. To them it must have seemed like a heroic adventure, with the travel glamorising the whole experience.

After a few weeks of searching for work, a friend recommended me to a hotel in Madrid centre, named 'Eurebilden', situated in the Paseo la Castellana, where I was offered a job in the restaurant.

One year later, I was bored with this, as there were no prospects, and I thought of going to France to look for something more interesting. I had the advantage, this time, of being able to speak the language along with my certificate of radio telegraphist in Morse code.

I explained to my mother that it was my intention to go to France, as I thought it offered better opportunities for me, and hopefully, prosperity which I knew Spain did not. She told me that she had known for some time that I was not content, and she was not surprised at my decision to uproot myself again. Nevertheless, she was saddened by my statement and said to me, 'I don't t know why you cannot settle down. With these adventures in your head all the time, I don't know how you're going to finish up in the future. But if you have to go, then you have to.' By this time, I was twenty-eight years of age.

I served my notice to leave the hotel and with the money I had and my passport ready, I went to Paris, two weeks later. I was a complete stranger in Paris. I knew no one at all. When I changed my Spanish money into French currency, I could see that it wasn't going to last very long.

The first thing I had to do was to get myself a room in a guest house. The woman owner asked me for one week's rent in advance, and after paying her, I was left with a small amount for food and other things. The guest house was in the district of Montmartre.

Every morning I went out to look for work. I was unaware that having served five years in the French Foreign Legion, I was entitled to resident privileges for ten years, which included weekly benefit for being unemployed and free accommodation by the French government.

In my ignorance of the circumstances, I was not claiming these benefits, which I badly needed then. And as my money ran out, the owner of the guest house asked me for another week's rent. I told her that I had only sufficient for one more night's stay, and she told me that I would have to pay her daily.

The following morning, I packed my belongings into my suitcase and went out on to the streets with no money in my pocket; just hunger in my stomach. I was desperate by this time, and it came into my mind that the only way to survive was to re-engage in the French Foreign Legion for a further five years.

My privilege with them had expired with the time lapse of the forty days from serving my previous five years with them.

I kept walking with my suitcase for about three hours; whilst wondering what to do, I suddenly found myself standing at the entrance of the Metro underground station, named Trocadero.

Continuing along this same road, something inside of me told me to stop and look at the church there. People were going in and out of the church, and I stood watching for about ten minutes before carrying on walking to the end of the road, where there was a bar.

I wondered if I could find somebody Spanish in the establishment who could perhaps assist me to find work. I stood there for half an hour, when two men, in their thirties, came out of the bar just then and stopped close to me, talking to each other in French.

However, as I studied their faces, I was sure that they were Spaniards. One of them departed, and the other one remained there, contemplating what to do.

Whilst doing so, he took a packet of cigarettes from his pocket and put one of them in his mouth. He then approached me and asked me in French, if I had a light. 'Yes,' I replied in French, and I took a box of matches out of my pocket and struck one, lighting his cigarette.

The stranger then asked me in French if I was waiting for somebody. I told him that I wasn't, but what I wanted to know was if he was Spanish.

'Yes,' he told me in Spanish. 'My parents are Spanish, but I was born in Paris.' I was very pleased to hear this, and I started talking to him, in Spanish. I told him of my difficulties, and he said to me, 'You're lucky that I was here, with my friend.'

He was sympathetic and gave me a cigarette. Then he told me to pick up my suitcase, as he was taking me back inside the bar for some coffee and sandwiches. His name was Vicente.

We talked over the coffee for about an hour, each of us relaying our problems to the other. 'Come on,' he said, afterwards. 'Let's go to the Spanish Church. One of the priests knows me.'

He led me back to the church where I had stood earlier, watching the people entering and leaving. Once there, he entered the sacred building, and I followed him. Vicente knocked on a door in a private passage of the church, and a priest soon appeared.

'Hello, Vicente,' the priest said, 'come on, in.' Vicente told the priest that he had come to see if the priest could help me in my difficulties. He told the priest I needed work. The priest invited us to sit down. He was very friendly and wanted to know what the problem was.

I explained to the priest in Spanish that I had come to Paris eight days ago from Spain to get a job and that I had found nothing and my money was all gone. Also, the owner of the guest house, where I had been staying, put me out on the street when I told her that I couldn't pay her the second week in advance.

The priest agreed that I had big problems. But then he said that he was sending me to an address where I could sleep only from 11.00 p.m. to seven o'clock in the morning. It was a private address, on recommendation from the church.

He signed a piece of paper, stamped it, and handed it to me. I thanked him, and he told me to go and see him every day and that maybe he could line up a job for me.

Vincente told the priest that he would take me to the factory where he worked. It involved a journey by metro, and on the way there, he explained to me that he was 'off sick' for two weeks with a bad back.

Having arrived, he then introduced me to some of his friends. Afterwards, I waited while he went to speak to the manager. Twenty-five minutes later, he came back to tell me that unfortunately, there was nothing available in the way of work.

I went to the guest house where Vicente lodged and left my suitcase there on his instruction while he took me to the address where I was to sleep. The place was within walking distance, in a private house, and after speaking to the caretaker, who inspected the paper which the priest had given me, I was told not to come before eleven o'clock.

Vicente took me back to the bar where we had first met. He bought coffee for both of us, and while I drank mine, he went over to chat with some friends of his.

Fifteen minutes later, he returned and said to me, 'Come on, Juan. We'll go to an inexpensive restaurant I know near here for a meal.'

Out in the street, he told me that a friend of his sometimes loaned him money. That friend was one of the men whom Vicente was speaking to, while I drank coffee, in the bar we had just left.

The restaurant was a typical workmen's place. Vicente ordered a meal for both of us and also, a bottle of wine, which was very cheap. For me, it was very enjoyable. When we had finished the meal, Vicente settled the bill and took me to see some more of his friends in a bar which I hadn't been to before.

This pattern continued for five days. I visited the priest every day, as he had requested in the hope that he might hear of a job for me.

By now, I was very frustrated, and I thought seriously of rejoining the French Foreign Legion the following day or even going back to Madrid. The latter was out of the question, though, because I didn't have the money for the fare.

However, on the fifth day, whilst visiting the priest with Vicente, I learned that there was no job in the offing; the priest had been making extensive enquiries on my behalf.

We left the church and outside, there was another acquaintance of Vicente. He was also a Spaniard, looking for work in Paris. His circumstances were better than mine. He was married, with two young children, but he had a house.

Vicente introduced the man to me as Mariano. He was a plumber by trade but unable to find a full-time job to meet his commitments. He was desperate and with no money to buy food for his family. So, he too, had gone to the priest for assistance.

Tile three of us stood on the pavement outside the church, talking for half an hour. Suddenly, a man, aged thirty or so, holding a small suitcase came and stood by us, listening to our conversation in Spanish.

He said, also in Spanish, 'Excuse me for interrupting, but after hearing you speak Spanish, I wondered if you could help me. I arrived here today from Madrid, and I don't speak French. I have a letter from my brother in the

Belgian Congo, telling me to go to the Congolese Embassy in Paris to arrange for me to join him in Congo.'

I read the letter that the man held out to me; then I told him that I spoke French and that I had served five years in the French Foreign Legion. After hearing this, the others wore an amazed expression on their faces. They didn't believe me, so I took the documents out of my pocket to show them.

Vicente said, 'I can't believe it. Why do you worry? If you go to the French government and explain to them with your papers, they will help you straight away with money, accommodation, and a job.'

I told him that I was ignorant about my entitlement. But, I was very interested in the stranger's intention of going to the Belgian Congo as a mercenary, helping the government of Mobutu.

He told me that with my experience and being able to speak French, it should be easy for me to do the same. So Julio, the stranger, Mariano, the friend of Vicente, and I went to the Congolese Embassy, leaving Vicente behind as he was afraid to go to the Congo.

We arrived at the embassy, which was not far away from the area of Trocadero. The three of us entered the building, and I asked one of the officials behind the counter if I could speak to someone in charge. He asked, 'Are the other two with you?' I said that they were. I was then told to wait while he went to fetch somebody, and he soon returned and asked the three of us to follow him through a corridor and on to another room, where it said 'Consulate' on the door.

We were called inside this room, where the gentleman sitting behind a desk, presumably the consul of the Congo, invited us to sit down. He was speaking in French and asked if he could be of help.

I went on to explain that Julio, who didn't speak French, had a letter from his brother who was a mercenary working for General Mobutu in the Congo. He wished Julio to join him there and instructed him in the letter to go to the consul in Paris to get permission and a contract to do so.

The consul wanted to know what qualifications we had. I told him that Mariano and I also wanted to go to the Congo as mercenaries. He said that it was a difficult and dangerous job. Also he enlightened us by saying that the job entailed using rifles to make peace between the rebels and the Congolese government and killing if necessary or being killed.

I asked Julio and Mariano if they were certain that they wished to go, and as Julio didn't understand French, I explained to him in Spanish.

Both of them assured me that they wanted to go to the Congo as mercenaries, and I had already made up my mind that I would go if it could be arranged. So I made this clear to the consul, who then asked me if we had any credentials or passports.

Mariano didn't have these documents with him, so he immediately went home in a taxi to get them. Julio and I had ours, so we gave them to the consul who looked at them, and when he saw that I had served in the French Foreign Legion, he remarked 'You are specialised in combat and armaments and also radio Morse code?' I said, 'Yes.'

Then he said, 'That is very interesting. We need people like you for our government.'

The consul then stamped our passports, with a visa of entry into the Belgian Congo. He returned them to us along with the other documents we had given to him and a contract for each of us to fill in. It stipulated one year.

He then told us to go away for an hour and complete the papers, glancing at his watch, which showed that it was 4.30 p.m. 'I will wait for you to come back,' he said.

Julio and I went outside the embassy and waited for Mariano to arrive. Shortly afterwards, he arrived in a taxi.

The three of us went to a cafe nearby. We had a cup of coffee which Julio paid for. Mariano told us that he had his passport and after having explained things to his wife, she'd agreed to his going to the Congo as a mercenary.

The two of them were nervous as they completed their contracts. But I was happy and very excited at the prospect of seeing the real jungle and its wild animals. It was a new adventure for me.

We helped Julio to fill in his contract, as it was all in French. And after this task was completed, we returned to the Congolese Embassy.

Once inside the consul's office, we handed back the completed contracts along with Mariano's passport, which was then stamped with a visa and returned to him.

The consul opened a safe, took out some money from it, handed the three of us twenty-five francs each and said, 'This money is to help you to get to La Bourget Airport. Tomorrow morning at eleven o'clock, you will catch a plane to Leopoldville, the capital of the Congo. On your arrival there, someone will meet you.' Rising from his chair, he shook hands with each of us in turn, wishing us good luck.

We went back to Mariano's house after leaving the embassy and gave his wife money to buy food for a meal for all of us. We slept at his house that night. The next morning, after getting ready, we passed the hours, discussing our new adventure until it was time to catch a taxi to Le Bourget Airport.

Mariano had promised to send money to his wife, before kissing her and the children goodbye.

On arrival at Le Bourget Airport, and after making enquiries with Air Congo, we established, when we gave our names, that our flight tickets had been arranged by the consul in Paris.

It wasn't long before we boarded the plane to Leopoldville, the capital of the Belgian Congo. The journey took seven hours; we had lunch on the plane.

When we got off the plane at Leopoldville an officer from the mercenary headquarters took us to the airport infirmary. After speaking to a doctor, he gave the three of us an injection against malaria, typhoid, and other tropical diseases.

The officer took us in his jeep to the mercenary headquarters, which was financed by General Mobutu, head of the Belgian Congolese government. On arrival, we were given a bed in a room with other mercenaries who were waiting to be told of their destination. Amongst them were Belgians, Germans, French, Italians, Americans, English, South Africans, and Spaniards.

In the headquarters, only the French language was spoken, which was officially used in the Congo.

When the men were sent to their destinations, they joined groups of mercenaries from their own country. This way they could converse with each other. Not all mercenaries spoke French.

My group had fifty Spaniards and was controlled by a commandant fully experienced in combat tactics. He was in charge of 1,000 kilometres of jungle terrain.

We remained at the headquarters in Leopoldville for two weeks. After being fitted out with dark green lightweight clothes and boots, we started training and learning the methods, which entailed the use of automatic Belgian rifles called FN. The ammunition magazines had twenty cartridges, and we each carried six magazines and four American hand grenades.

We were treated very well, during our stay here. There was a good dining room for the mercenaries and plenty of good food and beer. The black house servants waited on us, cleaned our clothes, made our beds, and so on. They were paid for their labour by the mercenary headquarters. My friends and I gave them a little extra money every day.

There was also a bar for the mercenaries, and there was no discipline at all. After six o'clock in the evening, you could go out into the capital to enjoy yourself but had to put your name in the book.

One day during the second week's stay in Leopoldville, while awaiting our destination orders, we were called to the commandant's office to sign the final mercenary contract which was for one year. The rules stipulated that you could terminate your contract after six months if you so wished.

The officer in charge gave Julio, Mariano, and me 12,000 Congolese francs and another 12,000 francs they put into a bank account in our names in Spain.

We were surprised and happy to find ourselves in the possession of so much money. The contract stated that if we were killed in action as a mercenary anywhere in the Congo, our next of kin would automatically receive 1,000,000 Congolese francs in lieu. But at that particular time, we were not thinking of that: only of the adventure ahead.

Cameras and taking photograph were not allowed, and any mercenary caught with a camera would have it confiscated. And as punishment, would forfeit his pay for a whole month.

It was on our last day in Leopoldville that a mercenary from the headquarters took us to the arsenal where all the guns and ammunition were kept. While waiting to receive my rifle and ammunition, I was very surprised to see huge iron spears which were made by the tribal people who lived in the jungle.

I took one in my hand out of curiosity. It weighed ten pounds minimum and was very long, at, seven and half feet. We were given an automatic rifle, eight magazines of cartridges plus ten boxes of extra ammunition for the rifle, and four hand grenades.

We slept that night at the headquarters and the following morning, four trucks with thirty soldiers from the Congolese army, accompanied by a truck with provisions and a Spanish Lieutenant mercenary, took us on the convoy, instructing the three of us Julio, Mariano, and myself to each board a separate truck, sitting next to the driver.

The convoy started its journey into the jungle in single file as the road was only wide enough to accommodate one vehicle at a time, with the giant trees closing out any view of the sky, even though it was ten o'clock in the morning. The temperature was at thirty degrees and reaching forties by the afternoon.

Our lieutenant told us that the jungle was very dangerous, and we could be ambushed at any time by the *Simbas*. These were people from the Congo, living well hidden, deep inside the jungle. They would kill for only one reason and that is 'matata mondele', which means 'kill the white man'.

When the lieutenant warned us of this, I put my finger on the trigger of my automatic rifle, ready for action.

It took us ten hours to reach *Lisala*, a collection of villages. One of the tribal chiefs came to welcome us. He was accompanied by about ten Congolese natives who were each holding a spear resting on the ground and several arrows were strapped to their backs with a bow across their chest. They were wearing nothing but loin cloth. The chief was a man aged thirty-five to forty years, and he was dressed in long trousers and a white shirt.

He spoke in French to us and while holding out his hand to shake ours, he said, 'White people, my friends. I know they come to help me and to civilise my people.' He invited us into his humble house, which was semicircle in shape and made from bamboo, sand, and water.

The Congolese troops had dismounted from their trucks and started speaking with the local people.

Our lieutenant informed us that we would be staying there for the night. The tribal chief gave us a meal of fried chicken.

Lisala was situated in Central Africa, which borders Sudan to the north and Angola and Zambia to the south. This was one of the areas where the Spanish mercenaries were keeping peace and order.

The tribal chief invited us to drink wine with him: a special brew that was milky white in colour, which was extracted from the Palm trees. It had a very unusual taste.

The villagers around here were slightly civilised by the white man. There were no shops to buy food, and they depended on what they could kill from hunting, such as elephants, hippopotamus, crocodiles, snakes, lions, leopards, buffalo, antelopes, and monkeys. Also large birds similar to turkey, and they also bred chicken.

We slept on the floor with our rifles in our hand. After hearing the noises from the jungle animals in the night, we woke up at five o'clock the next morning. After we got ready, we continued our journey along the river Congo for about three hours.

It started raining: a torrential downpour which lasted for about fifteen minutes. Afterwards the sun shone brilliantly and soon dried the road, which was of a terracotta colour.

After a while we were forced to stop our convoy of trucks, and the lieutenant went to inspect the obstruction and discovered a large tree across the road, blocking our path. He called us to go and to have a look.

I thought, after seeing it, that there was something suspicious, as one side of the tree had been cut with an axe. It wasn't the torrential rain that had felled it.

We called the soldiers to come down from the trucks and remove the tree from our pathway so that we could resume our journey.

Suddenly we were being shot at by machine gun bullets. It was the *Simbas*. The *Simbas* were the Congolese rebels who came from Tanzania, Zambia, and Angola. We were told of this by our lieutenant. These rebels were active all over Congo, attacking villagers who lived at the side of the main road. They would loot the villages, take the women, kill the men, and set fire to the huts.

The mercenaries were here to keep peace and kill the *Simbas*, but it was difficult to catch them because they were on the move all the time. Bullets were whistling around us, and we camouflaged ourselves behind the trees. I fired my rifle at random, as I was not able to see any *Simbas*. After about ten minutes, the lieutenant ordered for a ceasefire.

We went into the jungle, a little way, looking for rebels. It was difficult to walk in the undergrowth. The *Simbas* had disappeared into the heart of the jungle. Having removed the tree from the road, we then got back into the trucks and continued our journey for three more hours. We stopped in a village called *Ganga* for lunch.

The people here studied us with curious expressions on their faces. The men stood holding their weapons, which varied from spears, arrows on their backs, and knives. The women were bare-breasted.

We exchanged a few words with the tribal chief who spoke in Swahili. Not being able to understand him, we called a sergeant from the Congolese Army to translate to us in French.

It turned out that two days previously the *Simbas* had attacked the village, killing five men and taking six women with them into the jungle. The villagers were still afraid that the *Simbas* might return.

After a few hours, we continued towards our destination of *Bondo*, which was still two more days away.

Four hours later, we stopped at another village for the night and continued the next morning until we arrived at the river Congo. We crossed the river on a raft by way of the natives attaching a rope to each corner of the raft and pulling it to and from across the river.

It took two hours to get the trucks and the men across this way. The river was about 400 metres wide and some parts of it were 100 metres deep.

We arrived at *Kisangani* about 250 miles from *Kampala* in Uganda and about 200 miles from *Kigali*, in Tanzania. Kisangani is a very important town in the Belgian Congo.

We stopped the convoy here because it was a training camp of the Congolese Army who were instructed by the Spanish mercenaries.

Here, there were six Spanish mercenaries in charge of the Congolese Army training camp. We remained here for twenty-four hours leaving thirty soldiers and taking thirty new ones, including a sergeant in charge of a radio transmitter from the Congolese Army.

In the morning, we continued towards our destination. It rained heavily two or three times daily. Sometimes the wheels of the trucks would get stuck in the mud, and we had to push them out with great difficulty.

At six o'clock that evening, we arrived at *Dingila*. This territory is between *Kananga* in central Congo and *Bujumbura* in Burundi.

We stopped in *Dingila* for the night, where there were four more Spanish mercenaries. We gave them some food from our supply from one of the trucks. *Dingila* was a very dangerous territory, and the natives of the village were very primitive and completely uncivilised.

Aeroplanes couldn't land here because of the density of the jungle. Water was precious, and the women had to fetch it from the river and carry it back on their heads in pitchers.

Dingila had no hospital or medicine available for the treatment of malaria. Also there were no schools. It had a church with twenty European missionaries of both sexes, teaching and civilising the local natives.

Food was scarce here, and they ate what they hunted, supplemented only by tapioca, which grew wild and pineapple, maize, and bananas. They had no oil, milk, sugar, or salt and no spices either.

During our time here, we were informed by the Spanish mercenaries that the South African Army came into the Congo from South Africa across Zambia and Angola, killing the villagers and looting and destroying everything by setting fire. They also killed all the twenty missionaries.

They had no respect for the church either, which they destroyed along with the total destruction of the books, Bibles, and statues of the saints, which included Jesus Christ and Virgin Mary.

I was taken to the church to witness this. And I saw the devastation myself. I picked up the broken pieces in disbelief. The heads of the saints on the statues had been decapitated.

At ten o'clock the next morning, we continued our journey for a few hours which brought us to a large village called *Gango Bili*. It was fifty miles from *Dingila*.

We gave the Spanish mercenaries a few sacks containing flour, rice, oil, salt, and sugar and also, some tinned food. They were very glad of our arrival, as they had been without food for a week. They had survived on antelope meat hunted by the local natives.

We left two trucks and ten Congolese soldiers with them, and we continued our journey towards *Niagara*, about ninety miles away, which was our group's headquarters.

We stayed here for a month before going on to *Bondo*; we alternated between these two places and stayed a month at each.

We reached *Niagara* at eight o'clock that night having crossed another point of the river Congo, this time in a boat that was built by the Belgian engineers. This part of the river was about 600 metres wide, and it was dangerous, with strong currents. It was about 300 feet deep. You see hippopotamus swimming under the water and surfacing. Crocodiles were a common sight.

The mercenary group headquarters was 300 yards away from the river, surrounded by villages. We were welcomed by a lieutenant and eight mercenaries who were all Spanish.

The lieutenant gave orders to the Congolese sergeant to guide us from the trucks to his headquarters, where prisoners were held. These included *Simba* rebels.

We were invited by the lieutenant to go inside the sitting room of his headquarters, where we sat at the table and had dinner. The dinner was cooked and served by his servants.

After the meal, all the mercenaries chatted together, including the ones already at the camp before our arrival; there were twelve of us in all. We had brought them beer and food, and they were very happy. They were the first mercenaries to arrive in *Niagara* from the start of the Congo revolution two months previously.

We were later escorted by two of the mercenaries to our houses by the river, 100 metres away. These were European built, deep into the jungle. Each mercenary had a house for himself, although the decor wasn't very good. They were barely furnished, as they had been abandoned and looted a long time ago.

From my house, I could see the river and the native people in canoes, which looked like they had made by themselves from the wood from the trees. The canoes carried ten to twelve people sitting in pairs.

On our side of the river, there were always four Congolese Army soldiers on guard, checking the natives who came from the other side of the river with identification papers, stating that they were from *Niagara* or *Gangobili Lisala*, *Bumba*, *Buta*, or *Bondo*.

These documents were signed only by us. *Simba* rebels would come from inside the jungle without any identification paper and try to infiltrate the villages. They were from the *Bantu* and *Watutsi* tribes. Also, the *Fideles* and the *Pygmies*, all known to be cannibalistic.

Any white man being caught by these tribes would be killed, decapitated, and have their innards cut out and eaten raw.

We were specifically here to apprehend these *Simbas* or cannibals and to teach them to live a life in a civilised manner without killing their own people and missionaries working in that territory.

Next morning, we walked to the headquarters inside the jungle about 400 metres away and were welcomed by the Spanish Lieutenant and seven more mercenaries. The mercenaries totalled eleven altogether now.

Every morning at eight o'clock, the mercenaries and the Congolese soldiers would present arms to the Congolese flag in the presence of about 200 prisoners. These were made up of *Simbas* and other tribesmen who lived deep in the jungle. These tribes had no desire to be civilised by us or anyone else.

We handed over some of the prisoners to the Congolese soldiers to get them to cut the grass and tidy up the ground around the headquarters and our houses. The Congolese soldiers were on constant guard with a mercenary to issue orders to the prisoners. Other mercenaries patrolled the jungle with the Congolese soldiers.

The prisoners wore no clothes except for a loin cloth, and they had no shoes on their feet.

A few weeks would pass in this territory without any incidents; then the *Simbas* would attack the villages, and for this reason, we were on constant alert.

At night, you could see nothing except the small fire with four Congolese soldiers and one mercenary anticipating the next attack.

One particular night, I had been sleeping when suddenly at five o'clock in the morning I was woken up by the sound of shooting and screaming. I got up quickly and got dressed. Then I armed myself with a rifle and ammunition, including four grenades in my pockets. I went to the door and, in a crouching position, looked around to see where the shooting was coming from. I couldn't see anything. The sun was coming up, and it was getting brighter.

I went to one of the other houses, with my rifle at the ready. I shot two rounds into the air to alert my friend Mariano. He came out, asking, 'What's going on?' I told him the *Simbas* were attacking. He was already dressed and armed. We went to the headquarters, keeping our heads down as much as possible, while at the same time watching out for *Simbas*.

On arrival at our headquarters, the lieutenant said, 'Thank God, you're here. The *Simbas* are attacking us, and we don't know where they are. Take a truck, four mercenaries, and ten soldiers and go around the post to see if there are any casualties.'

He had been alone until we arrived at the headquarters. Soon we assembled ourselves and followed the lieutenant's instructions, taking a truck to one of the posts guarded by ten Congolese soldiers and a mercenary. We soon discovered the post was under attack by the *Simbas* from the noise of shooting; arrows and spears were also scattered on the ground.

We took position and retaliated with constant bursts of fire towards trees behind which the *Simbas* were hiding. I spotted them moving around, and they were shouting at us, 'Matata mingi mondele'; translated, it means, 'kill all the white men'.

We remained here for half an hour, shooting non-stop before ceasing fire. We then made our way carefully around the area to see what casualties there were but not before the rebels had retreated.

There were seven dead *Simbas*. Some wearing just a loin cloth, while the others were wearing the uniform of *Lubumba* Army. I noticed that one of the dead rebels had a rifle with the wrong ammunition, as the barrel was blocked. We collected all the rifles off the ground and buried the dead *Simbas* and also two Congolese soldiers who were killed in the attack.

We left four Congolese soldiers on guard with one mercenary. We returned to our headquarters and informed the lieutenant of what had taken place. The rest of the day passed without any further interruptions from the *Simbas*, so I returned to my house and went to sleep until the following day.

At eight o'clock the next morning, I went to the headquarters and was told by the lieutenant to take twenty prisoners, with five soldiers and go to the other side of the river to get long bamboo canes to put around our headquarters, giving it more privacy.

We crossed the river in canoes and walked for about one mile in dense jungle which was a very dangerous territory. We arrived at a village and saw the natives quickly retreating into their houses. They were wearing nothing but loincloth. It looked as if they had never seen white men. They were *Bantu* tribe, completely uncivilised, and they carried spears and knives.

I asked for the chief of the tribe in French but got no response. So I shouted and the chief came out of his hut, accompanied by half a dozen of his bodyguards. I approached him, with my hands extended, signalling him that we were friends and that there was no need for him to be afraid. I told him through an interpreter that I needed bamboo and wondered if he could help me. He said that he would send his men to get it for me.

The prisoners and three Congolese soldiers joined his men to go into the jungle to get the bamboo. The tribal chief invited me to drink some of his wine made from the palm trees. He was very friendly. He asked me if I would help him when his village is attacked by the *Simbas*. I told him not to worry and that we were there for that particular purpose. He then went on to tell me that they had very little food and asked me if I could get some salt for him. I replied that if he sent one of his men to our headquarters, I would let him have some and a sack of flour also. He was very pleased.

After three hours of waiting and listening to the tribal chief telling me about the ways in which they lived, the men returned with bamboo loaded on their backs. I gave the chief a few francs from my pocket, which he was very happy to receive. He asked me if I would go with him one day to hunt elephant with my rifle so that they could have meat to eat. I said that I would, and in return, he gave me five small ivory elephants, carved by himself. We left to return to the headquarters with the bamboo. I handed the chief a packet of cigarettes before we departed.

We made our way back through the jungle the way we had come until we got to the river. We loaded the bamboo on to the canoes and crossed the river. Once back at the headquarters, we designated a few *Simba* prisoners to the task of cutting the bamboo and erecting a fence around our headquarters. We issued them with knives for doing the job, and when it had been completed, we took the knives back from them and returned them to the prison.

A few days later, I was selected to take charge of all the armaments and ammunition, which we had accumulated from the previous attack by the *Simbas*. I had to pay special attention to this matter, as it was discovered that two Congolese soldiers were secretly taking ammunition and rifles and selling them to the tribal chiefs for hunting. They were punished for one week and made to cut the 'matiti'. This was the grass surrounding our headquarters. After this, they were imprisoned for a month along with the other *Simba* prisoners.

I was also put in charge of issuing permit documents to the villagers enabling them to go to neighbouring villages if and when they desired. The Congolese Army sergeant translated in French to me that many of the villagers complained of having no identification papers or registration papers from where they were born and also of having no hospitals or schools for the children.

Some of the *Simba* rebels had been educated in the capital, Leopoldville. I gave them permit documents signed and stamped so that they could go to other villages where they had relatives and in some instances, better living conditions.

A few days after this, our soldiers from the Congolese Army brought to me, at our headquarters, *Simba* rebels from the jungle, wishing to lay down their arms and join us.

I interrogated them, asking why they wanted to leave the jungle and the revolution against General Mobutu. The Congolese sergeant translated to me that they wished to be civilised and live a normal life, with their freedom obtained from us. They didn't want to continue the killing, destruction, and looting.

One morning, the prisoners were put on parade with the aim of delegating jobs for them to do. Two of them were given the job of being my personal houseboys, and the conditions were that they would not be returned to the prison but would be housed in a hut of their own.

The other mercenaries took charge of the other prisoners while I went to my house and explained to my two boys what they had to do each day. I was very friendly with them, giving them food and money, which they were happy to receive. One of them, whose name was Clemente, was able to speak to me in French. He had been educated in Leopoldville, and he was the son of one of the tribal chiefs of *Bondo* near *Bili*.

Clemente was a commandant *Simba*, fighting around this territory. His friend, my other houseboy, had been his right-hand man. They brought their wives to live with them, and they settled down quite happily. I was completely in charge of them.

One day, I told Clemente that I wanted a monkey for a pet. He told me that he would get one for me. He sent his friend, the other houseboy, who had done a lot of hunting along with some natives from the village to catch one.

They returned after five days and presented me with a very rare species of monkey called the 'macaco'. It was eighteen inches in height and had several different coloured markings. I named him *Kimbo* and soon discovered that he was very intelligent. Clemente told me that the monkey was about four years old. I put *Kimbo* on a chain for a week. Clemente brought fruits like bananas, pineapples, avocado pears, and melons from the jungle for him to eat. This was their normal diet.

A week later, I decided to release *Kimbo* from the chain. I told Clemente about this, and he said that he thought the monkey would return to me and not run away in to the jungle. So after giving him a banana and waiting until he had eaten it, I undid the chain and told him, 'You are free. If you want to go, then go.' *Kimbo* studied me for a moment and then dashed away quickly, disappearing into the trees. I thought that I had lost him and that I wouldn't see him again. Clemente and I waited for about ten minutes to see if *Kimbo* would return. Suddenly from out of the trees he came running fast towards me and from two metres away, he jumped right at me; I had to put my arms out to catch him.

I felt that *Kimbo*, my little companion, would remain with me for a very long time. I was right; he always stayed close to me. He was free to run around as he wished.

Around this time, the lieutenant ordered me and three other mercenaries, accompanied by twenty Congolese soldiers, to go to *Bondo* to relieve other mercenaries who had been occupied in keeping the peace there. And we were to take over from them and remain there for a few weeks.

The following day, we prepared ourselves for the journey and left *Niagara* in a convoy of two trucks and a jeep, which carried a heavy machine gun, and we made our way to *Bondo* through *Bili*.

I left Clemente and his friend in charge of my house until I returned. I took *Kimbo*, my monkey, with me. Clemente understood that the territory I was going to was dangerous and full of *Simbas*. He offered his services and the support of many imprisoned *Simbas* who had been previously fighting under his command. He said he would speak to them if I wished.

I thanked him for his offer but declined his help, telling him, 'Maybe next time, if I return from this mission.'

We arrived at *Bondo* three hours later, relieving the mercenaries, the Congolese soldiers, stationed there of their posts, allowing them to return to *Niagara* whilst we took over their duties.

The camp was situated at the side of the only road, which went through dense jungle. There was one detached European-built bungalow with four rooms to accommodate us four mercenaries. The weapons and ammunition were kept in one room, and the food was housed in another room. We lived and slept in the two remaining rooms.

There were six trenches surrounding the bungalow where the Congolese soldiers dug themselves in and guarded against any attack from enemy invaders who might encircle the place.

The following morning, I and another mercenary along with ten Congolese soldiers, patrolled the jungle, looking for *Simbas*, as we had been informed that they were making their own whiskey from the trees. This made them more savage and triggered off a spate of killing and looting in groups of thirty to fifty at a time.

We covered a mile in dense jungle and came across a clearing where we counted four barrels of whiskey and saw a few unlit fires. Close by was a large tom-tom drum. Suddenly spears and arrows started raining down on us from the trees and from behind the bushes. We opened fire with our automatic machine guns and rifles spattering bullets in their direction before going in search of them.

We saw them running away and shouting, 'matata mondele, matata mondele.'

There were some women and children around, asking us not to kill them. They were very scared. We took them back to the village with us and found out that the attackers were from the *Watutsi* and *Swahili* tribes. We returned to the site where the illicit whiskey was being made and destroyed everything.

We considered ourselves fortunate to have got back finally to the village without any injuries to us. We handed the women and children over to the tribal chief, not far away from us.

I had forgotten all about *Kimbo*. He spotted me from the window of the bungalow where he had been waiting; he leapt at me as soon as I entered. I was happy to see him; I gave him a banana.

A few days passed in this territory and then some *Simbas* came out of the jungle, handing over their weapons to us and saying that they didn't want to fight any more.

Food here was scarce, and we had very little to eat. We had to wait for the convoy, which brought the supplies from Stanleyville, 400 miles away. We received our supplies once a month, and that was the only means of transport, as there were no airports or landing strips in the dense jungle.

We were forced to hunt antelope. One mercenary and four Congolese soldiers would go out at four o'clock in the mornings, especially to hunt these animals.

We roasted them on an open fire outside our bungalow and found that the meat was very good.

The days here in *Bondo* followed a similar pattern with daily patrols into the dense jungle, looking for *Simbas* and anticipating attacks by them. We weren't afraid, as we had plenty of ammunition, and the armaments included an American lightweight cannon that could be moved by four men. It fired rockets that were about two feet in length and four inches in diameter. We had 200 rockets for the cannon, two electric bazookas, and three mortars, fifty-one and eighty-one millimetres.

We set up a post near the river, 200 metres front of our living quarters, guarded by four Congolese soldiers and one mercenary. This was because the *Simbas* were coming in canoes across the river at night. We kept our vigil all around the clock.

It was essential to sleep fully dressed in case of a surprise attack. *Kimbo* slept on my bed, gripping the headboard with his feet. He would wake me in the mornings by pulling at my ear lobes.

At five o'clock next morning, with the dawn breaking, *Kimbo* was very excited and started pulling my ear. I got up quickly and watched him jumping from one side of the room to the other. He finally stopped at the door standing upright, with his hands stretched above his head. I thought this was unusual and felt convinced that he was trying to tell me something.

Having dressed by now and armed with a rifle ammunition and hand grenades, I went out of the bungalow to inspect the guard around the trenches. Most of the soldiers were asleep. And I started to call them instructing them that they must never sleep while on duty. At that moment we came under attack by the *Simbas*. There were quite a lot of them, shouting and shooting at us. Within moments, we were completely surrounded by them.

As I looked ahead of me, I could see them criss-crossing as they advanced towards us from out of the undergrowth. By this time, another three mercenaries had arrived on the scene from the bungalow. They opened fire as they made their way to take up position around the other trenches.

The reciprocal gunfire became very intense, and I witnessed some of the Congolese soldiers camouflaging themselves into the trench in fear, not participating in the gunfight while the battle raged.

I told them, with my rifle pointed at them, to get up and start shooting and not to be afraid. At that moment, I noticed *Kimbo* at the side of me in the trench. He was clasping my legs with his little arms and whimpering with nerves at the noise of the machine gun fire.

I stroked him and said, 'Don't be afraid, *Kimbo*,' trying to understand how he felt, as I myself was feeling nervous at the time.

I put my rifle down and took hold of the heavy machine gun which wasn't being manned by the Congolese soldier in the trench perhaps because of fear and inexperience to use the weapon.

I issued emphatic instructions to one the soldiers, telling him to assist me by feeding the belts of cartridges into the machine gun, which enables the firing of the gun much smoother.

I was directing the gunfire towards the *Simbas* in a semicircular fashion, left to right and back again from right to left.

The enemy didn't let up in their attack on us, so I handed the machine gun control over to the Congolese soldiers, who, by this time, understood the handling of it. I eased myself out of the trench, taking a Congolese soldier with me and positioned ourselves into the adjacent trench. I took hold of a 51 mm mortar which was already in the adjacent trench. There was plenty of ammunition for the mortar. I needed the soldier to assist me with the mortar's ammunition. The range of the mortar was between 50 and 200 metres. I fired mortar towards the *Simbas* into the jungle.

The fighting continued for about half an hour, and then the enemy stopped shooting and retreated into the jungle. Suddenly it went all quiet.

I, with another mercenary and ten Congolese soldiers, went on a patrol in the area where the *Simbas* had been fighting. Ten dead *Simbas* were discovered, and there were four injured, who were bleeding from their wounds. We buried the dead rebels and took the injured ones to the bungalow. I sent a message by radio to our headquarters, asking them to send transport to fetch the wounded for medical treatment. I also requested more ammunition for our armaments, as we'd been under heavy attack from the *Simbas*.

Juan Rodriguez—1965 aged 29

It became a routine for the *Simbas* to mount an attack on our position at least once or twice a week.

One day, early in the morning after a torrential downpour, a mercenary, eight Congolese soldiers, and I, along with eight natives from the local tribe, crossed the river in four canoes. The jungle on the other side was *Bili* land where no white man had previously been.

We saw hippopotamus and crocodiles in the river. Some of these animals were on the bank of the river and quickly submerged into the water as we approached near them. The natives asked us to shoot one of the hippos for them to eat. We agreed and shot one of them in the head with our rifles. The hippo appeared a mile or so down the river as it didn't die immediately. The natives started cutting the flesh from it, and after taking it back to their village, they would smoke the meat over an open fire to preserve it for weeks to come.

Also, the other mercenary and I killed a crocodile that was resting on the bank of the river. As soon as it was hit, it dived into the water to take cover; like the hippo, the crocodile was caught further down the river, where it had got caught up and entangled in the tree branches and foliage.

We walked for a while and came across 'signals' of tree branches which were tied to upstanding trees. On the ground were branches which had purposely been laid in crosses. The natives informed us that it meant anyone going beyond would be killed and eaten.

The other mercenaries and I laughed when we heard this and took no notice as we continued on our way, breaking up the signals in our path.

We carried on walking for another hour or so and arrived at a village where there were a few primitive houses made of sand and bamboo. There was nobody to be seen as the place had been abandoned and some houses had been destroyed by fire.

I picked up an ebony carving, the bust of a woman, from the ground and kept it for myself. My friend also found a carved figure. After looking around for a while longer, we turned and headed back to the bungalow.

We headed back to the river and crossed the river in canoes. Moments later, back on the land, we were being attacked by spears and arrows and saw a hundred or more tribesmen charging towards us. They were shouting, 'matata mondele' over and over, which meant' kill the white man'.

We immediately opened fire on them and ran towards the road which led back to our bungalow. I looked around, and it became apparent that I was on my own. The natives and Congolese soldiers had disappeared into the jungle; so bad my comrade, the other mercenary.

I continued running towards the bungalow, looking back every now and then to see how far the enemy were. I dropped my ebony carving in haste to escape.

After running for about 550 yards, I was exhausted. I arrived at one of our posts on the side of the bungalow. I explained as quickly as I could get the words out, to the mercenary on guard and four Congolese soldiers to hurry and take position in the trench situated in the middle of the road because tribesmen had attacked us from the bank of the river and were chasing me.

Having camouflaged ourselves in the trench, we saw the enemy coming towards us with spears and knives in their hands. We opened fire and threw hand grenades. The enemy soon dispersed into the undergrowth on both sides of the road. I remained here for about fifteen minutes before returning to the bungalow.

On arrival at the bungalow, I explained what had taken place to the other mercenaries. Whereupon, I and another mercenary and twelve Congolese soldiers, fully armed with ammunition, returned to the scene of attack near the river.

We searched for my friend and the Congolese soldiers who had disappeared. We spotted a group of tribesmen near some trees with knives in their hands and some flesh. We opened fire on them and continued shooting for a few minutes until they fled.

We moved forward for a closer inspection. Nothing could have prepared us for what we saw lay in front of us. They were the mutilated remains of the torso and the clothes, which had been torn apart, of the mercenary who had disappeared while we were being chased by the tribesmen.

It was a sickening and horrific sight for us to endure. Nearby were also the remains of the five Congolese soldiers and three native hunters' bodies who had befallen the same horrible fate. We never discovered the rest of the group who went out on the hunting trip with us.

The rifles of the men, who had been butchered, were taken by the cannibals. We buried the Congolese soldiers and the native hunters in the jungle; we took the remains of the mercenary back to the headquarters. By this time, the truck from *Niagara* had arrived with food and ammunition. We put the four injured *Simbas* aboard the vehicle, including the remains of the dead mercenary's body, and it was returned to *Niagara* for a proper burial.

During the days which followed, we were on constant guard. Nobody was permitted to leave the bungalow and a few days later, we were attacked again by cannibals. There were about 200 of them shouting at us while throwing spears and shooting arrows. A few bullets were also being directed at us. The rifles they used were those stolen from the soldiers at the time of the body mutilation. This time we were prepared. We opened fire on them and set up the cannon firing rockets towards them: six in all. The impact on them was too much, and they soon disappeared. We ventured out in search of them but saw no trace except for a few dead ones lying around on the ground.

I remained in *Bili*, some three miles from *Bondo*, for a further week. Towards the end of that week, early one morning, two trucks with thirty Congolese soldiers and six new mercenaries arrived in a jeep to relieve us of our duties. We informed them of the attacks on us by the *Simbas* and the cannibals, warning them to be on constant alert, especially early in the mornings.

We gathered together our personal belongings, not forgetting my pet monkey *Kimbo*, who had been so pleased to see me on my return from the battle near the river.

On the way back to *Niagara*, the Congolese soldiers started singing. Further along the road, natives from the burnt and looted villages were making their way to a rehabilitation centre with their belongings on their backs. They waved to us, knowing that our presence there gave them a little more security. They lived in fear of the *Simbas* and the other tribes.

When we reached *Niagara*, we gave the lieutenant the details of what had occurred in *Bili* and of the dangers. He said that he was glad to see us still alive. He then went on to tell us that the butchered mercenary had been buried respectfully and his next of kin had been informed.

We were given permission to relax and to return to our houses with instructions to be back on duty the following morning. I took *Kimbo* home and on my arrival, I received a welcome from Clemente, my house servant, and his assistant. Soon afterwards Clemente said, 'Buana, I've got some hot water, for a bath, ready for you.' I asked him how he'd managed get hold of a tub. He told me that he'd found the tub in one of the houses abandoned by the Europeans. He'd cleaned it in the river and brought it back to my house. The water was from the river, which he'd heated in an old metal barrel on an open fire.

I was pleased with Clemente's gesture, having not had a bath for three months. We normally washed ourselves in the river, fully aware that there were crocodiles around. One mercenary would keep watch on these occasions.

I had my bath and was glad then to be able to relax in my house with *Kimbo*. Even while relaxing, I had to keep my pistol with me in case of sudden surprise attack by any of the local native tribes.

Clemente brought me a large bag and said, 'Buana, I have brought this for you.' When I opened it, I saw that it was dried tobacco leaves. He told me that it was the tobacco they smoked in Congo, and that it was very strong. He said he would be able to bring me some every day.

I rolled some of it into a cigarette from the papers I had in my attaché case and after smoking one, I felt completely relaxed for about three hours although still aware of what was happening around me.

Clemente brought me another present: two ivory tusks which had been carved by his grandfather who had died sometime previously.

I asked why he was giving them to me. He said that I was a good man and he didn't want me to go away. Also if I had been a bad man, they would have killed me and eaten me. By they, he meant the cannibals.

A meeting was held at the headquarters the next day, which I and eight other mercenaries attended, with the officer in charge discussing the general conditions and the situation of our camp.

The food supply for us as well as the Congolese soldiers was almost gone, as the convoy which delivered the food from Stanleyville to our camp was attacked by the *Simbas* on its second day of departure. Six Congolese soldiers had been killed along with two mercenaries who were bringing fresh supply of food and ammunition.

When the Congolese soldiers came to us, asking for food, we had to tell them what had happened, but some of them had doubts and refused to do guard duty, saying that they wanted food and would have to go into the jungle to hunt for some. We gave half of them permission to go and hunt and told the rest of them that they would have to do their guard duties, guarding the prisoners. If they refused, we would kill them.

They held a brief meeting amongst themselves, and afterwards, one of the Congolese sergeants came to us and said they had agreed upon half of them going into the jungle to hunt animals every day until the convoy with the food arrived.

We were in the same situation as they were as regards food, but now we had to double our guard for our own protection against them since they had become aggressive and very dangerous.

A few days later, after having explained these matters to Clemente, he offered to help me. I asked him how he could help. He told me that he was one of the big chiefs of one of the villages in the jungle: not *Simbas* or the cannibal tribe, but just natives living their own simple lives.

He said that with the help of some of the prisoners whom he knew and some of the natives, they could go hunting for us but unsupervised, promising that the prisoners would come back with him.

I took Clemente to our headquarters and explained to the lieutenant what he had told me. The lieutenant thought it was a good idea provided his word could be trusted.

After being reassured of this, the lieutenant offered ten prisoners and two rifles with ammunition. He then gave Clemente 2,000 Congolese francs, asking if it was sufficient to buy chicken from around the villages. Clemente said that it was, and he told the lieutenant he was pleased that he had confidence in him.

I went to the prison with Clemente, and he selected ten of the prisoners, who I called out to line up. Clemente spoke to them, in Swahili, on the way to my house, explaining what they had to do and at the same time, impressing upon them that he had given his promise to the mercenaries that they would not run away.

I gave one rifle to Clemente and one to his right-hand man. After shaking hands with Clemente, he said to me, 'Buana, I will send chicken for you tomorrow!' Just as Clemente had promised, two natives brought eight live chickens to our headquarters on the following day, and we roasted three of them on a fire out in the open. We were, by this time, without cooking oil.

Next day, Clemente sent a blue antelope with two of the prisoners he had taken with him. The following day, Clemente sent a large bird that looked like a turkey, but it wasn't a turkey. We were kept supplied for a week.

After a week, Clemente returned with the prisoner. We still had several live chickens in the yard. Clemente said he couldn't get any more chickens as the other villages were too far away and so he returned.

The lieutenant thanked him and let the ten prisoners remain free to hunt for us in the locality.

I brought Clemente back to my house. The prisoners built huts for themselves nearby. Clemente would instruct the prisoners to go hunting daily; on one occasion, they brought us an antelope.

This is how we survived, as the convoy carrying the food still hadn't arrived, three weeks after it had been due.

On one occasion, Clement suggested to hunt an elephant and the lieutenant agreed to this, as the prisoners and soldiers were very hungry.

Julio, the friend who had become a mercenary at the same time as me, arrived from another zone known as *Buta*, where he had been keeping the peace with other mercenaries and soldiers. It was his turn for a little relaxation.

He told me this place was paradise compared to *Buta* and *Ganga Bili*. I told him things were not so good here, as we had been without food supplies for three weeks owing to the fact that the last food convoy had been attacked and destroyed by the *Simbas*.

I asked Julio if he wanted to go on a hunting expedition to catch an elephant with us the next day. He said, 'Yes, I would like that.' He was excited at the thought of it.

I gave instructions to Clemente to prepare the ten ex-prisoners ready for the following day's hunt, and I ordered four Congolese soldiers to prepare themselves with rifles and sufficient ammunition for a week.

Early next morning, seventeen of us set off towards the river without having any breakfast. We went in five large canoes down the river, stopping briefly now and again, looking for traces of where the elephants had been eating.

After an hour, we stopped and put the canoes under the trees to camouflage them. Clemente told me that some of the men had spotted evidence of elephants having been in the area recently.

We walked in double lines into the undergrowth, using machetes to hack our way through. The ground was very muddy making it difficult to walk. We stopped to rest occasionally, and the hunters were setting animal traps. By this time, we were very hungry and had used up extra energy, getting through the jungle and perspiring profusely.

We didn't have much luck catching an antelope either but were grateful for the pineapples and bananas which were growing around.

We came upon a group of banana trees, and everyone was helping themselves to the fruit. Julio and I were happily picking the bananas, not seeing the danger which was lurking there. Clemente came dashing over to us, calmly saying, 'Stop, don't move.' He pulled aside a large bunch of bananas and exposed a python which was wound around the trunk of the tree.

I was ready to shoot it with my rifle, but Clemente said not to. Then he called two of the hunters with the knives, who stabbed the python and cut its head off. They took it from the banana tree, skinned it, cut it up in pieces, and cooked it on skewers over an open fire.

Clemente gave Julie and me some of the cooked snake to eat, but after some hesitation, we managed to get it down us and found the pinkish-white meat acceptable, whereas the others clearly regarded it as a delicacy, licking their fingers afterwards.

We slept that night in the jungle and lit a fire as a deterrent to any wild carnivores roaming in the area.

The following morning, we continued our journey in search of the elephants towards Lake Tanganyika, in the direction of Tanzania. We came across a family of lions, and there were also zebras, giraffes, gazelles, and buffalo grazing nearby.

The hunters picked up a trail made by the elephants, which changed our course back towards the river. After walking for about three miles, the hunters told everyone to slow down and to remain quiet. If a group of elephants felt threatened, they would charge towards you.

Thirty or so elephants were grazing from the trees, and we got as close as possible to one of them, waiting for it to face us so that we could take aim and shoot it in the head.

Julio and I fired a few shots at the elephant's head. After it had been hit by several bullets, the elephant collapsed and died. As soon as the other elephants heard the shots, they ran away.

We walked over to the dead elephant. The *Simbas* and the Congolese soldiers began cutting away at the flesh and afterwards, carried huge pieces of meat away on their backs.

I took one of the elephant's tusks and Julio took the other. The group then turned and made our way back to the canoes; having unloaded the meat, the hunters returned to the mutilated animal to strip more flesh from it, assisted by four Congolese soldiers.

The hunters and the soldiers were singing and were very happy with the catch, saying to me, 'hoo hoo hoo buana' as they rowed the canoes. I asked Clemente what it meant, and he told me it meant I was a very good man.

After two hours on the river, rowing against the current, we arrived at our headquarters. Many natives came to help carry the elephant meat to the headquarters where the lieutenant distributed the meat amongst them.

I returned to my house afterwards with Clemente. Kimbo leapt at me excitedly in total surprise. He looked very happy at my return.

The following day, when I reported to the headquarters, the lieutenant asked me to interrogate two cannibal tribesmen who the Congolese soldiers had caught in the jungle. I sat at the table and told the Congolese sergeant, who spoke French, to bring the prisoners to me for questioning.

As they stood before me, I studied them. I found them to be different in appearance from any other Congolese natives I had seen. Their stomachs were distended, like a seven-month pregnant woman's. They wore large ivory rings through their pierced ears, and their mouths were wide with lips of unusual thickness, their bottom lips turned over. They wore ebony rings around their upper arms.

I told the Congolese soldier, in French, to ask them why they killed people and why they killed white men and ate their flesh. The Congolese sergeant spoke to them in Swahili. They replied that they didn't want anyone to interfere with their way of life. I told the sergeant to ask them the second time why they ate the flesh of humans. I wanted to know this. They told the sergeant, after he had questioned them again, that they believed that having eaten the flesh of the white men made them ten times stronger.

I ordered the sergeant to take them away and put them in prison. The sergeant said that if he did that, the other prisoners would kill them. I asked the sergeant what he suggested should be done with them. He said that the punishment in these cases was to put them in a hole in the ground thirteen feet in circumference and thirty-two feet deep. They were thrown into the hole and left to die without any food or water. This was the punishment for the *Simbas* if they were caught after escaping. I witnessed the two men being thrown into the hole, on this occasion, and that was the last I saw of them. A guard was put around the hole to prevent them from escaping. They would be shot if they tried to.

A week later, while still in *Niagara*, three mercenaries and I took a jeep and went on a patrol of the surrounding area of our headquarters. We stopped the jeep by the road, got out, and started to walk into the jungle. After about 200 yards, we came across a church believed to be built by the Belgians. We went inside to have a look. All the contents in the church had been destroyed. One of the mercenaries came upon a hole in one of the interior walls. From the hole, we could see another room.

We broke through the wall and entered the room. There we saw two trunks. We opened them up and found they were full of Congolese money. We took the trunks and headed towards the jeep, but as we left the church, we heard voices and saw a huge number of men-eating tribe coming towards us, throwing spears and shooting arrows.

We quickly dropped the trunks on the ground and positioned ourselves to fight back, taking cover. We fired a few rounds of our rifles and hurled a few grenades at them. When they heard gunfire, they stopped in their tracks. We made another attempt to retrieve the trunks and load them in the jeep. As we ran carrying the trunks, the spears and arrows started flying towards us again.

It was a struggle to reach the jeep. One of the mercenaries was hit in the back by a spear, which went right through his chest. He fell to the ground and died instantly. The trunk of money he was helping to carry to the jeep also fell to the ground.

One of my comrades asked for help in getting the dead mercenary's body into the jeep. While trying to lift him, the natives were coming towards us still hurling spears and arrows at us and were getting very close.

We had to leave the dead mercenary and one of the trunks in a desperate bid to escape with our lives. We managed to get one trunk into the jeep. I set up the heavy machine gun, which was in the vehicle with the help of one of the other mercenaries.

The driver of our jeep quickly tried to reverse the vehicle in the opposite direction which led to our headquarters, while I discharged a hail of bullets towards the rapidly approaching natives.

The driver zoomed away up the road at high speed towards our headquarters. On our arrival, we explained to the lieutenant what had occurred. He was very upset at the news and ordered twenty Congolese soldiers and six mercenaries to take two trucks and a jeep to the scene of the attack and bring back the body of the dead mercenary.

When we arrived at the location, we looked around and found that the body of the mercenary had been taken away by the natives; just the blood where he had fallen could be seen. The second trunk with the money was still there, untouched. The whole group of enemy had disappeared. After a thorough search of the area, we found the mercenary's clothing, torn apart and spread around.

We returned to the headquarters; after reporting our findings to the lieutenant, I went to my house.

I received news that Mariano, one of the other mercenary, who came out to Congo with us, had been severely injured in a heavy attack by the *Simbas* at a place called *Ango* near *Bondo*. He was taken to Stanleyville hospital. I was informed of this over the radio, and it was the last I had heard of him.

Julio, my other friend from Paris, was fighting in *Gango Bili* where there had been many casualties. I heard over the radio that the survivors of an attack by the *Simbas* had escaped into the jungle.

By this time, the fighting in the Belgian Congo between the white mercenaries and the *Simba* rebels was getting very fierce. All the mercenaries, including myself, fighting in the *Niagara*, *Bili*, and *Bondo* areas were getting scared and frustrated because of lack of reinforcement, food, and ammunition. We were becoming dependant on the food that the hunters could bring us.

Another week passed before the convoy of trucks carrying the food, ammunition, and more Congolese soldiers arrived. They brought four new mercenaries with them.

I returned to *Bili* for another month where the pattern of attacks by the enemy was similar as before, two to three attacks a week, but at least, we had food to eat and more soldiers.

We had to do patrol duties around the areas of *Bumba*, *Monga*, and *Bondo*; these areas were unknown to us. The natives, who had escaped into the jungle at the height of the fighting, started to come out and build houses near us for protection. They were very much afraid of the *Simba*. Some of them gave the mercenaries gifts of miniature carved ivory elephants.

The attacks from the *Simbas* started to slow down to about three a month. About 400 natives from the jungle had set up homes around us by this time. As a security measure, we were asked to check their documents, as it was understood the rebels were merging in with the villagers.

Reinforcements arrived to relieve us of our duties; we returned to *Niagara* and filed our report to the lieutenant. I went to my house, after filing my report, where Clement and Kimbo were waiting for me. There wasn't much to do around here now.

It was October, and I was in my eighth month of being a mercenary. It was very hot, with occasional torrential rain that lasted for about fifteen minutes.

We made a few more expedition into the jungle to kill elephants and hippos for the resident natives and Congolese soldiers.

On one occasion, on my way to the headquarters, with Kimbo walking in front of me, he suddenly turned and leapt up on me, gripping my neck with his little hands. I said, 'what's the matter, Kimbo?' He was very nervous. I looked in front along the road and saw a fifteen-foot long black mamba, making its way across the road. I aimed my rifle and fired a few rounds. The snake continued on its way and was out of sight. Kimbo wouldn't release his grip on me and held on for dear life. I went to investigate to see if I had killed the snake; I couldn't see it anywhere.

Late in October, a message came over the radio, asking us whether we wanted to relinquish our duties as mercenaries or continue with them. I decided to leave Congo. I had seen enough, with the food and ammunition delays and our comrades being eaten by the cannibals. The conditions were, in many ways, too much to contend with. We had been ignorant of these facts at the time of volunteering for the job as a mercenary.

Two months later, in December, it was time for me to depart but not before being involved in several more attacks in *Bili* and *Bondo*. Clement brought about twenty pounds in weight of locally grown dark brown leaves, which the locals smoked as tobacco. It was a departing gift, but I told Clemente I didn't want it, as it was overpowering and also I wouldn't be able to get it through the customs. The police were very strict in searching the baggage, sniffing for drugs and confiscating them; if found guilty, you could be put in prison. Cameras and films were also confiscated.

Clemente packed a small elephant tusk with some of the tobacco, unbeknown to me. It wasn't until I returned home to Madrid that I discovered it. He also brought a phial of gold nuggets which came from his family's mine. He said he would bring me more everyday if I would stay. I asked him where the gold came from. He said it was a secret and only he and his family knew the location.

We waited a week for the transport which would take me and four other mercenaries to *Dingila*. From here, we went by an aeroplane to an airport near Lake Tanganyika, close to *Katanga*. We caught a large American transport plant to the capital, Leopoldville. After a further week of waiting here, we were handed over to the mercenary headquarters in Leopoldville.

We had to stay in the headquarters for two more weeks. Then almost by surprise, a mercenary officer arrived to tell us we were to board a plane to Madrid. It was the twenty-fourth of December nineteen sixty-six. It was ten o'clock at night when we boarded the plane. We arrived in Madrid on the twenty-fifth, the next day, which was celebrated as Boxing Day in Madrid.

As I got out of the plane, I saw the police searching everyone. A few mercenaries had bought elephant tusks as mementos to bring home from their adventures. I brought some ivory also for my mother and grandmother. They were very surprised to see me having come through dangers that involved both *Simbas*, who were rebels fighting against General Mobutu, and other wild tribes, including the pygmies.

My mother and grandmother were both crying with happiness and to see me alive again. I was also crying with happiness and to still be alive. The tusks I brought as souvenirs for myself formed a part of the collection that I had from my previous adventures in Africa.

I stayed with my mother in her house for a few months but during this time, I started having nightmares about the *Simbas* in the jungle, chasing me with long steel spears, which I could almost feel in the back of my neck, as they gathered speed and my feet seemed rooted to the ground, not able to escape from them. They were obviously intent on killing me while it was my intention to stay alive.

Those terrifying nightmares continued for many years, and I dreaded going to bed at night because of those nightmares and the 'Simbas' who invaded them.

After my marriage, even my wife would be woken from her sleep because I would repeatedly 'scream out', frightening her because she had no idea what was causing them. She would then 'shake me', telling me to 'stop it', but it wasn't easy stopping those 'nightmares', as they put me back into the 'Congo', where 'men' really are eaten.

The End

Juan Rodriguez

tructions:

is a brief questionnaire for our Book Video Services. Please take the time to answer ALL questions
oughly to ensure the highest quality representation of your book. When you are finished, save the
ument to your computer, attach it to an email, and send it to the email address from which this
ument was received.

se enter the title of your book:

" THE CONGO WERE MEN ARE EATEN, "

vide your name as it appears on the book, along with pronunciation:

se note that if you have ordered a Premium Video and do not provide the proper pronunciation of your name, the voice over
e recorded with our best possible guess and an additional fee will be incurred if it needs to be re-recorded)

JUAN RODRIGUEZ.

se provide a brief description of the location and time period in which your story takes place.

IN 1966-67. IN THE CONGO"

fly describe the main characters in your book. Please include basic visual appearance (ie.
der, age, ethnicity, hair color, any major defining characteristics.) We will try to accommodate specifics
r as our resources allow.

My private help - Name Was Clement,
a coronel, Simba, cature By the congolese
army inside the jungle, aswell, he was about
24 - years old, heir Black, he told me, that he
want to help me, and Was With me all the time, he
Was speack speck France, and he Was doing
For me, traslaition of their languis,
aswell With me was a small maca.co with four
colours, Very intelegent, he Was the same a human
been, one day save me of a Bait from one snake,
he Black Bamba, Full of poison,
e snaik Was kill, by my body gard,

Enter a one-sentence hook line that will grab readers' interest. For example, "A fast-paced thriller in which a former spy relies on his old skills to save his kidnapped daughter."

HERE YOU WILL SEE, ACTION, MISTERIOUS,
THE JUNGLE WITH ALL THE DANGER -
I HAS TO SAY - THAT I WAS FAITING SEVERAL
TRIBUS - CANIVALS, FISELES, pigmis
SIMBAS, AND REBELS - REBELS, AGAin

Please provide a clear, detailed synopsis of your book. GENERAL MOBUTU.

-If your book is **fictional or based on a life story**, this should include a brief description of t
beginning, the conflict that stands in the way of characters reaching their goals and the
resolution/conclusion to the story.

-If your book is **non-narrative based** (i.e. poetry, self help, educational etc.) then please prov
few paragraphs describing the main points and themes you'd like to get across in the video.

WALKING inSide THE jungle, just me, and
10 - soldiers from the Congolese army,
I was with my Rifle automatic, aswell, with
10, petacas of reserve around my Belt, about
200 bulis in reseve, I has to fite canamivals that
in that moment they were ataking us, with
arrows, and Big javalines, make by them, very
fevy, of pure IRon, going every where, to cuch
any of us, I told the soldiers to hide themself -
my rifel automatic open fire to all this canivels
that come from no where, the soldiers,
I don't know were, disipering, and the canivels
no stop, making a lot of noise, HAAAA, HAAAAA,
Haaaaa, mondeles, mondeles, I got, one of my
granades, and throu to them, they got, a
soprise from me, and they stop crying Haaaa,
I through about 3 - granades, and all the
canivals, dissipere, and I start to look,
for the soldiers, but only come out 4 - the others
gone, For ever, this was the Congo, 1967

Book Video Questionnaire

Instructions:

This is a brief questionnaire for our Book Video Services. Please take the time to answer ALL questions thoroughly to ensure the highest quality representation of your book. When you are finished, save the document to your computer, attach it to an email, and send it to the email address from which this document was received.

Please enter the title of your book:

" THE CONGO WHERE ME ARE EATEN."
By JUAN RODRIGUEZ.

Provide your name as it appears on the book, along with pronunciation:

(Please note that if you have ordered a Premium Video and do not provide the proper pronunciation of your name, the voice over will be recorded with our best possible guess and an additional fee will be incurred if it needs to be re-recorded)

Please provide a brief description of the location and time period in which your story takes place.

The location of my story start in The capital of Leopolville.

Briefly describe the main characters in your book. Please include basic visual appearance (ie. gender, age, ethnicity, hair color, any major defining characteristics.)

Today the name is KINSHASSA. here in the capital I was destine, to A Head cuaters of Belgian merce. nary. here they give A BED, and I has to stay here, For 5 days, they give me and uniforme, as A mercenary, everything was here, very similer, of te military fort, every morning a group of merce- ary, was doing sport, for about half and hour, ien they was calling you the their office, and they rt to do or the particulars, about you, and king you everything, about 12 AM. We has to site any of the tables, where there, and in the restaurant stort to know the others mercenarys, around , they were as well voluntaires Same me, here I w them, they were voluntaires to get a very good omy every 15 days, or 30 days, they money was in ngolese money money, I was here with 4-more romiards, from Madrid - Spain, and from paris, well voluntaires, recomend it, secret, I engage n Paris, after I was doing interprete, in FRENCH,

because I new the French languis
i was speacking very well the languis,
in French, the Consulate Congoless, ask.
me, if I would like to go the to the Congo,
Working for General Mobuto and help, the
soldiers, Congoleses, about How to working
with the arms - the gusil - the army congole
Don't understan verywell, anyway I say yes,
and the Counsel, or embass-der, in paris, ask
ing me, I say yes, only per one year, they tole
me ok, and they give a little money to spen.
Was the money very very good, I Was no spect,
all that, money he give to me, aswell the two
spanish men that they came from Madrid,
recommend it, from somebody - but they whasin
speek speak, any French, I has to do, the
conversation in French to the to two 2-
spaniards, anyway I continue here in lec
polville, the capital, for 5 days, here we
eaten very well, and the waiters they give to
everything serving by them, every day, and
was very happy, with the things was coming I
do know nothing, till the 5 day - 3 lorris, tra
they were prepere, with ammunicion, for the a
aswell one of the lorris was Full with, flawe
aswell with sacks of RICE - and other food
in lates conserves oil, Salt, sugar, and few
more things of Food. then after they prep
all, this they told us, that we can go,
the DESTINACION - about 2.000 milles, to
South of the congo, and the North of the
Congo, all Real fugle, very cick cick, with
trees everywhere, and big plants, but, the
Sargont Congolesse, was-telling me in Frenc
that we have to go, in very danger territory

... ... to be very _3_ alert, of everything.
Were to see, the raining of the water never finish.
e time we have to get out of the lorry, because in
out of us was a big tree accross the rute, and the
ris has to stop. all the people remove the tree,
+ was very febre, and the water no stop, aswell, tornen
rute, and no finish yet, because now we were ataq
the Simbas rebels, that they were in this territory
oubangui, accross no far awey the river Congo
there, every-body was camuflash, bittain the
trees and big plants, bulis were going everywere
u can file them, pass by, aswell, some arrows, I
start to be on my gard, and look every where
see the Simbas, that sometime you were liesen
ein to scrimen with voices, Hummm, Hummm,
stop, many of the congolesta army they were
plitibly camuflash, and you don't see any
them, they were very afreit, but me, I was
ry relaxe, con mi falo automatic, 20 bullise
catrisse, petaca, that, carry the bullise, I can't
e nobody, all they were well, camuflage, and,
ne, anywere, from now on I say to myself, I has
look to myself, because this stupids, congolesse.
ldiers, they dissipere, From were I was, bikain
big tree, and look for them around, 15. minuts,
were from ataque, and no stop, after stop - my
nds the three spamars come out, a little affreit, with
t Happen and we talk about the ataque Simba,
new they want to take the food, and everyting -
- We put them out, to the fungle, we never show
m any more, the rain hasen't stop, We continue
- rute, 3 soldiers dissepier into, the fungle,
d few Boys from the Kinshassa, that they come
h us, in our lorris, of transport, after another
ours of rute in the transport, we arrive to
other village, Name, Bateke land territory,
stop here, few minuts, South of Sudan,
ross Shangha River, infesty with Crocodiles
and Ipopotanos, Hippos ...

Enter a one-sentence hook line that will grab readers' interest. For example, "A fast-paced thriller in which a former spy relies on his old skills to save his kidnapped daughter."

Please provide a clear, detailed synopsis of your book.

-If your book is **fictional or based on a life story**, this should include a brief description of the beginning, the conflict that stands in the way of characters reaching their goals and the resolution/conclusion to the story.

This book is fiction and is a sequel of the first book Dollars & Diamonds, so Liquid Diamond picks up from where Dollars & Diamonds ends.

-If your book is **non-narrative based** (i.e. poetry, self help, educational etc.) then please provide a few paragraphs describing the main points and themes you'd like to get across in the video.

Where is your book available for purchase online?

Amazon, Barnes and Noble

For example, www.amazon.com , www.barnesandnoble.com , etc.

the river Congo in a Big canoe made by them, to go accross this RIVER CONGO - We h to put one by one of the lorris, this was a Big We try to pull the Big canoe, with rope the one sid to the other side, a lot of working we did, then continue our rute, and after few hours we stop the rute, and we slip in the side, we make fire and after we went to slipe, till the about 5- oclo in the morning, and we continue our rute, few-tim we has to stop in the middle of the rute because the lots lorris stick in the math with water, and was very difficult to get out of the hall, every loa has to pruss the lorry one, by one, some time in the rute we have to stop, because we come accr with a family of elephants, the soldiers on want to kill one of them for the meat for the we give the orden, of not to kill, any of them, ou they continue inside the jungle, without an more trouble, this people, want to kill any of them, but we told them, no, no, no,

www.xlibrispublishing.co.uk

Victory Way,
Admirals Park
Crossways
Dartford
DA2 6QD
United Kingdom

P

ress Release Questionnaire

By affixing my signature below, I am authorizing Xlibris to fulfill my press release.

Book Title:

Project ID:

MR. JUAN ARGENTA RODRIGUEZ.

Juan Argenta Rodriguez

SIGNATURE OVER PRINTED NAME

Date: 11/06/2013

- 6 -

after 5 days inside the thick jungle we
arrive to our destination, that was with
the name, of ganga, no far away from
BONDO - many Simbas, Canibals,
pigmis, and otrer tribus, were
situaity here, arround ganga,
re was my Destination, very Far from
Leopolville without, help from any
ody, only 8 - Spaniars, with, 20 Joldiers
From the congolless army - Some of them
Don't now how to put a bulley in the rifle,
nd anotherthing. going away into the
jungle went was an ataque by the Simbas
hey were very afreit, some of them, they
lere sit in the grown, with the two hans
n the top of the Hed, very afreit,

here in ganga_ no faraway from lissala_
and lussaka, territory without know anything
yet, because we were the ones, has to go to there
and civilise people, that they never, see,
a white man, so when they start to come
out the inside the jungle, and start to make
the houses for them, with mug wet, and bamb
and in the top of the house, big libs of palmier
tree, after they start to live happy neers us,
for any help, an away from the simbas, and
the canivals no faraway from our head
cuters, one day in reconaisansse, me, my bo
gard, the name clement, well educate from
the university in Leopolville, was speak w,
me always in French languis, went to joing,
x the simba army full of people, against
general malutu, revellion, many, many,
clement was telling me everything, he was
a comandant simba, capture by the
congollesse army and bringe to us, as a
criminal, rebel, simba, in our prision
that we has here, & in ganga, in this prisi
were 400, prisioners, simbas, criminals, pic
mis, canibals, an other tribus, so, every me
ning we were on parade in our head cuters,
in the GANGA, put the flag congollessa, up, every
were there every morning about 8. oclock, AM_

the spanish capitan, from andalusia, the south a
spain, and 8- spaniars, and 400 prisioners, wer
there, after one sargent, distribut it, 10-or 12-pri
ners, were going to cut Bambu, to do thing around
te camp, I got 10 of them, chusse by me, an one of t
was clement, other was a coronel simba, freind o
my body gard, clement, because I give him his liverty_
for all his working, for mi, and the translation, fr
their languise to me in French languis, I was the on
spaniar was speaking in French, I was very imp
for the transleation, one day two soldiers broug
to my office one of the canivals, capture by the
soldiers, in front of me, and they told me that thi
canival, eat, flash of the white man, I ask Him why
eat it the flesh of the white man, and he
that he give them the

After the 3 day, We arrive, at another Village, the name Was, Gango Billi, A not to Big Village, But very Danger, the Simbas, and the Savages canivals they were around, and they re ataquing few times, into de bouses, of the rmal people living happy, but they had to many ataquts, and now they were very afreit to y in the villages, some of them disipiers, to ther Villages trough the jungle, Waking - re we stay For the night, slipe in the villages, they were 4 - Spaniars living here With them, one radio operaiter From he Congolese army - profesional, because yself new the Work of radio telegrafic. the French Foreing Legion, e nest day We Went, again with our lorris transport, aswell we have have a gipp. merican gipp, We left food, and armunissio, then, and change 4 - congolesse Soldiers another 4 - of the ones were coming se us, From Leo-pol Ville, things they were very good in this territory - Was very Danger, t We continue our rute, to get our stination, the radio Were We were going as saying that they haven't got much food eat by radio, because one of the congolesse diers, Was radio telegrafic, and he aswell old me in the French languise, I start to understand, all the trouble around here, d very danger, to many rebals Simbas ere against general Mobutu, so for us. he 12 - Spaniars they were here sitnaity it, Few Villages Were in real Danger

8

Today here in our Head Quaters in
Ganga - no faraway Frone Bondo - a
village very dangereus, because many SII
REVALS, they were living around here, aswell
around this territory were, canivals, real ca
nivals, that they pute you in the cacerole, a
& EATE you, thee same if you were an anima
they don't know about you, and never see a
white man, we were watching by them, behaine
the big trees, and plants, we don't know, an
ting about them, but me went I was stay fe
one month here in the our head Quaters, my
boy help, the comandant - SIMBA - REBALL) - sey
to me, that one of the canivals that was capture
By the Congolesse army soldiers, one day tha
I was in charge of this prisioners, that we cap
re, inside the big junge, I was site in one cha
and I has a Board taible, two army soldiers com
in with this Camival, a little fat, and with mo,
cloths at all, only an scuere rope around his par
and the two 2 - soldiers left about two - 2 - or 3 - meter
in front of me, and I start the questions to the
camival, and I asking him, why his other canival
Kill one of the white men, and after they eate Him
the same an animal, and him say to me, that
we eate the white man, because, when we eate
the flexsh of the white man, we get the force, of
10 men, the two soldiers congolese told my Boy
gard, that he was speak with me in FRENCH,
languis, told me everything, I say to the 2 -
soldiers to taken him to prison, with the others

is was onother day of, my stay here, in
anga, my monky & the name Kimbo, was
eeways with me, a very small monky-macaco 3
y colorful, green Hielo, white green, & black, and
ite, was very special monky, capture, from the
einds Simbas of my Boy gard, that I give orthen
utorisation, to him, to go to the jungle, and get
e monky for me, to stay with me, he say to me
s Buana, he always call me BUANA-) and
y to me that will take him a week, to get it,
say to him yes, ok, and in the 4-day, he brought
me, and he say to keep him gard because maybe
cape, I got a chain, and I put to his body, with,
force, and I give him, bananas, melon, payapple,
d other food abaibivl, around here, one day
at was the 4 day with, me, I put out his
ain, and I give him his liverty-and after
say to him, Bay, Bay kimbo, you are to go,
nd him straight away, he show himself free,
e went away very soon into any of the trees,
they were, around here, and I say to the Boy
ard- now is free, he can go with the others,
monky, and Clement, that was his name say
o me, Buana, kimbo, will be here in a
nimuts, or neva, and was truth what he
ay to me, because kimbo, come from the
rees, straight to me, and always, he was with
e, everywhere, FREE, he was very intelegent
monky, macaco.3 he was very gaung, about
1 years old told me Clement

this day after we up the flag in the morn
a group of 3 spaniars, and I, my monky K
and my Boy the name Clement, we has to go o
in serch of something inside the jungle, aswell, 1
congolesse soldiers, come with us in serch for Simba
or pigmis that they were around, look for white m
aswell, we ask few of the Boys help, to come with us
carry 2 - machines automatics, as well, one mor
of 81, very fevi to courrie, in a quarter an Hour,
left the camp, and we went into the intense ju
about 1-mille wouk, we stop in one of the fa
From the trees right in front of us in the flore,
was retten with pess of cotton, and seid, that if the
mondele go across, this signal, they will kill all a
us, but we don't take it serious and we continue
wok. accrosse, then about 10, minusts, big arrow
very fevee, of iron, make by them, was coming from
one of the sides, of the trees, everybody straight awa
take camuflasse, I an my monky, with me, as well
Clement, say to me, they are simbas, and
Carnivals, mix, I start to give orthers, to the so
diers, to start to put, the machine gun and
start to shut open fire, but this soldiers, conge
lesses they are afreit to open fire, some of them
they dissepier already and the heep Boys, aswell,
an the flore, with don't know what to do, this was
another ataque by the Simbas and carnivals,
chaiting very Hig, mondeles, white men, my rifle
automatic, was fire all the time to were I thought
the were bihind the trees, and plants, my monky
was all the time with me, aswell afreid of all the noise,
after Half and Hour, things went very siloce,

Went to the new destimaition, was a territory
camp By us, and we has to gard it, 24 hours a day,
re was, very, very, Danger, here the Simbas, were
ery where, Because they were living around here,
side the jungle, and here where we has to stay for
re month, in the morning we went, with A GIP.
merican gip, me, my monky Kimbo, 3 spaniars,
ll with our automatics rifle, amunitions, for
Camon no very big, was made by China, amunition
By America, in big boxes, and 12 soldiers, congolle
res, from the ARMY congollesse, we has to show them,
ow to Fire with their rifle, because they were coming
oluntaires from Leo-polville, because was a Big,
demand, By General Mobutu, all of them, has to
aken orthers from us, aswell, we has points were
ny people, want to go, to another village, or
nother, City, or town, has to have a document,
ign by us, in our Head Queters, camp, we has
well with us one lorry of trans-porte, only for
ur use, nobody eles, they has to have our permision
nd sign a document, We arrive in about 2 hours,
ecause the road here is all mug, and very diffi-
ult to drive, and more difficult, when was raining
verybody change plaices, and the spaniars aswell, in this sector, of territory we have about
o-miters visible, without any trees, or plants,
ou can see if enybody aproch, but from bittaind
f our house that we has here, we all trees, and
lants and you can't see anyting, we were al -
ays on the looking, because the carnivals,
he simbas, and pigmis, they were no very far
way, We allways has 2 soldiers, on gard,
ow I am going to say, that food for us,
nd the soldiers, they were given a little rice

73-

a little salt, and a little lad, oil, not
~~olos,~~ else, food allways very in demand f
everybody, one spaniar was allways in gar
about all the food we has for one month but
always we were, sort of food, the camp were we were,' was m
than a Fort, we told de soldiers to diging in the g
right in the midle, about 10-to-15- milers all free of
nts, and any tree, all was very clean, in the midle, we
have small Hols, were to put the amunition for our r
and aswell to to camuflage yourself from the Sime
and others tribus, Camivals, pigmis, Simbas, F
they were to many mix all togeather, we ~~hafe~~ have,
around our House ~~tt~~ trinchera, with A machine gu
and plenty amunition, our House were slip the 4
Spaniars was full of amunition, aswell we have
plenty amunitions, for the camon, we can put the car
any were we like, ~~p~~ because was no ~~heby~~ Hevy, and 3-or
men, can muve the camon, every day we watch, the
congolese soldiers, doing the gard around the cam
they were very Happy, because we left them bring
ing their wife, and the wifes, they was doing the
lunch for the 12-Congollesses, soldiers, and the
day, we were teaching them, all about how open
fire, with the rifle that we give them, the rifle
in this days were of one bulli, only the 4-spa
niars have the automatic rifle, with, 6-to-8-
petacas, of 20-bullis each one, we always has
the automatic rifle with us, at all times, aswell
we have, 4-bomns, BONBE,) american, we call them
painaple, very good, aswell, we have here with us,
2-Bazakas, and two-2-mortiers, one-81^M.
the other was, 51^M. that niely every day we has to
working ~~the~~ with the two mortier, because the "SIMBAS
and other tribus, they start to atague us, in the
morning, about 5^AM- the ~~ataques~~, were about,
½ half an hour, some time we has to use the

e around here, was very danger, to be alive,
t we continuing day by day. and after
s no more fire, we went to see what casua-
tes they were, very few, because, constante
ze, from both mandos, # this day about
oclock AM in te night, my momky, the
ame Kimbo, was taking my EAR, up and down,
n was with his small body- towers my head,
d he was no stop calling me all the time till
pen my EYES, and I show him look to my EYES,
d he was chat Hiiiii, and Hiiiii, and start to —
lamp, up and down, he want to tell me something,
s new, that was his message to me, we the 4- spani-
rs, always seep, with the trousers, and the boots,
n, very soon soon I put my cinturon, with
ry petacas of ammunition, 4- Bombs, and my
utomatic rifle, that was neres me, and I went,
traightaway out, and & give the alarm, to the
trers 3 spaniars, and very soon, we went, to
he trincheras, with the Hols, and very soon,
iriting for the Simbas that in this moment
hey were all of them around all of us, camu-
lash Bihaind the trees, and plants, 100 hun-
dre of them, or more, everyting was very silen-
ie, and you only can see, the clarite of the moon
Butt was not full moon, sudenly, the Simbas,
tart to ataque us, just light that, the soldiers,
some of them don't xx know what to do, they were
panic, but we has to start our fire, straightaway
with our automatics rifle, aswell, we brought
from our house the two mortiers, with plenty of
ammunition, and the # 4- spaniars, including me,
start to worcking with the 2- mortiers without

stop, tronghing the Bombs, I went to
machine gun because the congolless
soldier, don't even start, it, because
of the bulliss, was stop in the midle of t
canon, and I has to use my skill, of the forein
legion, and put the canon of the machine g
in correct orthen, I start to shut every w
                                        avery
without stap for a few minust, after that, th
noise of the bulliss slowdown, and we have
time to put things, right, aswell, the spaniar
in charge of the cheina canon, was com
to the centre were we were in this momen
and we start to help him to put the Big
catriss, ready inside the canon, we trou
about 4 of them, one to the left into the
jugle, one to the right, aswell to the jungle, a
two 2 in direct line, the noise, of the Fir
the canon, was incredible, suffissant For
all the Simbas, and Camials, working wi
them Vamus, dissipeere, away to Direction
(. BONDO,) a big village with everybody
over there, they has to go accross the river
congo to arrive to BONDO, about, 5 killometres,
they went accross the river, in piraguas, lon
ones, that marking themself from the good tr
this was another day for all of us, day bye
my days in the congo belga, today leop.
ville.) Kinshassa, Brazzarbille, and men
others citys that I was,
the days was coming to and END 30 days

16

EVERY

We were 3 weeks already here, and ~~everry~~ every soldier with us were very happy - to finish ~~4~~ the 4 - weeks, - but in the last week to be here, on the next two 2 - days, in the morning about 9AM - 2 - Spaniars and I, went on our - jeep, to see anything around our head quaters ~~here~~ here were we are, no faraway from "BONDO" we went, the Simbas, and canivals, and other tribus, around here, we were ataque by, minimu 50, canivals, in the forest of the jungle, we were looking for a church that was here, about 2 - killometres, from our camp - we were wo-oking were was the church, we new that was no faraway- church that was ataque by them, and killing - or 4 - sisters from the church, aswell, 2 - prist, from the church, aswell all the figures of the, church, the Virgen Mary, Jesus, and others saints, ll were broken, and everything else, that were ere, nobody new why kill the Humans as the sis - rs, and the two 2 prists that they were here to ach them, and prey with them, as civilise, eople, but they don't want to understand, nd one day, kill all of them, we were no far - away from the church, and we went to see, if as something important to take with us, to the amp, and we left the jeep, in the road, and, after been woking for about 50 meters, we were ataque by the canivals, trowing arrows, big ones, nd spiars, we start to retulate to them with ~~ot~~ e our rifles automatics, that we allways, has ith us in all mudments away any were, he canivals was coming out from the big orest, pass from one side, to another side, and chanting to us very strong, we has to go back to our jeep, car, runing, and baking.

around, to see them coming behind us
to kill anybody, very angree with their voices, one of the spaniars, went down to the
grand, ground, my monky was with me in the
hombres nerest my Head, around my neck, with
his to Hands grasp, to my body, very afreid, and
We were aswell, and with one of the spaniars
in the flor, ground, with one of the arrows, in
his body, and the canivals no stop coming to
us, our Rifles were working all the time, but
very difficult to get any of them, we don't know
how many of them went to the grown,
I think few, with all our bullis, to stop them
but they were all the time around us, bet wi
the trees, we arrive to our jeep, and straight
away we went, we were like that our jeep. car
was in the right direction, we went very fast
away, and when we taed the other spaniard
and the soldiers, congolese, we went back ag
again to get the spaniard that was kill, with
one of their arrows, big one, made by them, o
iron, and if any of them tuch your body, the
arrow go into your body, if catch you in yourbo
We arrive there, to get the spaniar, we were, abou
30 people, with all the Help, straight away we sho
half body of the spaniar, no legs, no arms, no head
all dissipere, to the jungle, the canivals, took with
them for what, I tell you for what, was, to EAT. his fee
put in the fire, and vurnt, and after that, they ke
the meat for very long, same the mojama, in spani
languis, anyway, we got his small dorse, of his body
and in few minutes, the congobless soldiers, arrive
with 2 - Canivals, that they got from inside the jung
Were we were, we ask them what happen to the legs

nd hans, and Head, the Sargent congollese, Was

king to the two 2 carnivals, with no cloths,

nly, small + pess of lather, on under, his body

ey say one of them, the same thing, my brothers

vant to eat the White man because, after that,

hey get into their body, very strong power, the

orce of $10. men, that was why they took with

hem, everybody of they, and dissipere, into the

jungle, we back, to our camp, and put he

alf of the body of the spaniar, into the ground,

and venie him, and Give him, three_3_ Fire with

our rifles, and put him with a croixe, in "GANGA"

e rest of the week, Was very sentiment, the congollese

soldiers, Put the two-2-carnivals, in prision,

with the others, more th down, 400, prisioners,

I Would like to put all I said, in my Book,

the name," THE CONGO Were men are eaten,

— Juan ARGENTA RODRIGUEZ.

www.ingramcontent.com/pod-product-compliance
Lightning Source LLC
Chambersburg PA
CBHW030129260626

47156CB00008B/2855